SIMON PARISH

CLOSED SEASON

Bolero

First Published by Bolero Books 2002

ISBN: 0-9538452-1-4

A catalogue record for this book is available from the British Library.

Bolero Books is an imprint of Plum Tree Publishing Limited, Worcester, England, WR7 4NX

Printed and bound in Great Britain by Omnia Books Limited, Glasgow

Closed Season

1

I met Rebecca Waters on my first day at Oxford. It was her feet which first entered my field of vision as I bumped up the stairs with my heavy suitcase, then the sturdy legs pushed into tight jeans followed by a generous bust and finally, as I reached the top stair, an even more generous smile.

"Hello, I'm Beck."

"Phil," I volunteered, gasping for breath, "Philippa James."

"Here, let me give you a hand," with which she relieved me of my case and proceeded to help unload the car, assembling a growing pile of belongings in my room; a simple act of kindness yet typical, as I came to learn, of a warm and giving nature. I took a liking to Beck straight away.

The spontaneous invitation to coffee in her room after my father had left was equally in character. With a head start of two days, she had succeeded in creating order out of chaos and producing a homely atmosphere from the most unpromising of materials. It was here, over the next three years, we were to spend long nights hotly debating the burning issues of the day and where, on that first occasion, I learned something of my new friend.

Beck came from East Sussex where the family home was a large, Georgian house, and her father was a G.P. with his own practice. A housewife and magistrate, her mother was also a keen gardener - in fact, Elisabeth Waters' garden had even featured in some of the glossy magazines. Beck had in a sense followed in her mother's footsteps by applying to her old college, where she had been welcomed with open arms and offered a place on the strength of an interview and a report from the head of her private girl's college. Her choice of PPE was prompted by a desire to enter the world of journalism, specialising in political reporting.

For my part, I told how my father was Chief Design Engineer for a manufacturer of textile machinery in Nottingham where we also lived. Ours however was a modern, mock-Tudor house on an executive estate. I couldn't recall any particular hobby of my mother's although she had worked at the local lending library before bringing myself and my brother Mark into the world. My place at Oxford had been gained through a scholarship from the grammar school following my A-level results.

Given such different backgrounds, it is difficult to explain why we subsequently became such close friends; after all, the differences between us far outweighed the similarities. Beck, for instance, was pretty in a cuddly sort of way whereas I am basically just plain. Her shock of rich brown hair contrasted with my lank, mouse-coloured locks and her fresh complexion with my tired, pale skin. Intellectually too she was in a different class and her First never seemed in doubt whereas my Upper Second in History and English was the product of much midnight oil and was never a foregone conclusion.

But my friend's achievements weren't just confined to the academic sphere. She was a dedicated and accomplished oarswoman too and it was she who introduced me to rowing, and through rowing to Sara. My own skills at rowing took longer to acquire and at first I caught more crabs in an hour than a Cornish fisherman in a whole year. But with time I came to master the techniques of a sport which gave Beck so much pleasure and which came to play such a large part in my life too.

After graduating, Beck unsurprisingly landed herself an enviable job in the editorial section of Current Affairs at the BBC. There she rubbed shoulders with many of those household names, reporting nightly on our screens from the world's trouble-spots and acquired contacts, which were later to prove invaluable in our self-imposed task.

For my part, I found it impossible to obtain any job at all, let alone one to which I felt my privileged degree entitled me. Returning to the parental fold, I lay fallow (as my father sarcastically put it) for a while, before embarking on a series of casual jobs, which brought a degree of financial independence. At the same time, I had a base from which to apply for a permanent job, the nature of which became less and less critical as time went on. But the fledgling had really outgrown the nest, and there was frequently an undercurrent of tension at home.

My first serious job offer came just as things were nearing breaking point. Before the interview, I had never been to Milton Keynes, and no doubt there are many decent, God-fearing citizens living out honest lives there. But it was not a town which featured in my top five hundred most desirable places in which to live, though this was simply prejudice on my part. My opinion did not change after that first visit.

The job of graduate marketing trainee with U.I. Foods seemed the ideal opportunity. The company car made the decision all the easier, in fact the decision-making process was purely notional. Let's face it, I didn't have many options.

Responsible for overseeing my budding new career was the Assistant Human Resources Manager, Richard Tonks. 'Rich', as he asked me to call him, seemed to have reached his own personal career plateau some years ago, but he was not unlikeable. Before aspiring to higher management, he patiently explained, I would first have to acquaint myself with the business from the roots up, and would spend six months in the apprentice training school, learning the rudiments.

This introduction heralded one of the unhappiest periods of my life. Never before, nor since, have I felt so lonely. Starved of intellectual stimuli during the day, I would return to my solitary digs at night, to a diet of convenience food and television. How I longed for the companionship of Beck and my other friends from Oxford, even for the warmth and creature comforts of the parental home. At every opportunity, and without fail at weekends, I would flee what had become my self-imposed hell.

But there is a God in heaven, after all, and this purgatory was cut short when, after just three months, I was promoted to the position of Marketing Consultant and allocated my own territory.

It was as a direct consequence of my new role at U.I.F. that Beck came to play an even more important part in my life than she had at Oxford. Given my new-found financial security, I decided to buy my own place, to become a proud mortgage-owner. (Despite the vagaries of the property market, my father was still a firm believer in the bricks-and-mortar philosophy of wealth creation. Why pay rent into someone else's pocket, when that self-same money could go towards buying your own house? he reasoned. Get your foot on the ladder! No dot-coms for him.)

I chose not to live on top of the job but to settle somewhere fairly central, yet west of London. Commuting to my allotted territory shouldn't be a problem, not with the new improvements on the North Circular, I reasoned. And so I came to settle on Shepherds Bush - the less fashionable part. After Milton Keynes, the colour and bustle of the Uxbridge Road was a constant source of fascination - the people, the cosmopolitan restaurants, the news-stands selling papers from all over the world, the shops stocked with everything from picture hooks to yams.

The flat was, in fact, a maisonette, purpose-built around the turn of the century, with its own front door. It was just one of hundreds like it in the terraced streets off the Uxbridge Road, but to me it was home.

Beck at that time was sharing a house in Twickenham with four other girls. The arrangement was satisfactory at first but, with time and the addition of two live-in boyfriends, things had become fraught. So she leapt at the offer of my spare room and within days we had set up home together.

The Flotsam Rowing Club, as the name might imply, started out as something of a joke. It was founded on the Thames by a group of Oxford graduates who wanted to row for pleasure, rather than in competition. Almost inevitably though, they became caught up in the competitive tide and began to enter races at regattas. Never brilliant, they were, nonetheless, always to be found in the top fifty at the Heads of the River race. At the same time, they never lost sight of their founding principals, and maintained a clubhouse and bar second to none. It was here, as a new member, that Beck introduced me to Sara.

My first impressions of Sara were not favourable. She was surrounded by a small circle of admiring studs, plying her with a disgusting combination of drinks. Sitting on a stool at the bar, her skirt, short to start with, had ridden up round her thighs and she seemed to be somewhat the worse for wear. Although pleased to see Beck, she was more interested in playing to the male gallery than meeting me. Some time later, our Captain, Barry, persuaded her to participate in the activities of the Club in the fuller sense, and not solely in a social capacity, although our treasurer, in presenting the accounts at the AGM, jokingly held up a blown-up graph, showing how the takings from the bar had plummeted, since Sara took up rowing, and spent less time propping it up.

The turning point in my personal relationship with her came when she stood in for Sue in our boat one day. Fortunately, it was only a practice session, but hard enough, as we were entered into a regatta next day and this was the last opportunity to get our act together. I remembered how painful, literally, my own initial outings had been and my heart went out to Sara, as she made all the mistakes I had made and, like me, paid for them dearly. It was I who, uncharacteristically, took her under my wing, as Beck had with me, guided her, protected her from the criticism of others and, not least, told her how to treat her painful blisters. My initial opinion of her - as a mindless bimbo - changed, as hers doubtless did of me, and a friendship was born. With time, she came to apply the same single-mindedness to her rowing as she did to her pleasure seeking. A well-worn cliché, but Sara really did live life to the full and got a hell of a lot out of it in return.

Educated privately at a select school for girls in Malvern, she had gained a Third in modern languages at Exeter, following which Daddy paid for a bi-lingual secretarial course at a private Oxford college. There, it was inevitable, given her startling good looks and bubbly personality, that she should be drawn into the University social scene, and eventually into the boating fraternity. The same qualities coupled with her classy accent meant that, on moving to London, she immediately picked up a plum job as personal assistant to the MD of a small firm of public relations consultants.

It wasn't until some weeks after meeting Sara for the first time, that I became aware of the existence of Rupert - we had only ever seen Sara on her own at the Flotsam clubhouse. (Rupert's sole appearance there had apparently not been a success. For whatever reason, the boating fraternity had denied him their seal of approval.)

The occasion of our first meeting was a dinner party at Sara's flat. There, he was unexpectedly introduced as her flatmate; I say unexpectedly because, even at that stage, there had been no prior mention of his name. But that wasn't the only strange thing - the whole set-up seemed decidedly odd.

On the second floor of quite a smart house off Notting Hill Gate, the flat was clean and tidy, even if the furniture showed signs of wear and tear. After the initial introductions, Sara showed us into the sitting room whilst Rupert disappeared to organise the drinks. First impressions do generally count, but I completely failed to form any clear impression of him from this first encounter. Having served the wine, he immediately disappeared back into the kitchen with hardly a word, whilst Sara entertained us with small talk, accompanied by Gregorian chants, popular at the time, on the CD player. In due course, we were summoned into the kitchen/diner where Rupert had clearly been preparing the meal, and a very good meal it was too. Excellent smoked salmon, served with asparagus, preceded veal ecalopes in white wine and mushroom sauce accompanied by fresh pasta and a dressed salad of raddichio, fennel and roquette. A superb selection of cheeses and a zabaglione followed, for those still able to do them justice, which included me. The meal was complemented by a dry, white Bordeaux with a claret to go with the cheese, though Rupert apologised for being unable to offer a dessert wine with the zabaglione. We were impressed.

Throughout the entire meal, he fetched and carried while our gracious hostess remained ensconced in her chair at the head of the table, and entertained her guests. He spoke only the minimum necessary, glancing at Sara frequently for any signs of assurance and praise, however faint. These, Beck and I lavished on him in good and well-deserved measure but, although blushing slightly, Rupert refused to come out of his shell and stayed behind in the kitchen when we retired to the sitting room for coffee.

Before leaving to go home, I felt it expedient to make a trip to the loo. Passing down the corridor, I mistakenly opened the door into a small box room, where I nearly fell over Sara's rowing machine. The remaining space was taken up by a push-bike and a number of suitcases. Besides this room, the adjacent loo, the kitchen and sitting room, the flat contained only one further room, serving as a bedroom. Could Sara and Rupert possibly share this room, or did he sleep in the sitting room? There was no evidence of it doubling up as a bedroom. When he finally returned from the kitchen, I looked at him in a new and more critical light.

"Funny little chap," remarked Beck, after leaving. "Do you suppose there's more to that relationship than meets the eye?" she pondered.

"Doubt it," I responded, and meant it. I didn't mention the mystery of the sleeping arrangements; after all, I could have been mistaken - wine can play funny tricks on the mind.

I clearly remember our second encounter with Rupert. Although doubtful about our ability to match the culinary excellence of Sara's hospitality, we felt obliged to reciprocate with a return invitation. Some weeks later therefore, Sara and Rupert duly arrived on our doorstep. This time, Rupert was dressed in the now familiar outfit. The strange, mustard-coloured trousers I recalled from our first meeting, but the most striking feature was the long, knitted scarf, from which he refused to be parted despite the warmth of the evening.

"It's his little comforter," explained Sara, with a knowing wink.

Rupert took this and other little taunts from Sara in good heart. But as the evening wore on, his confidence grew and, spurred on by Beck and myself, he began to fight back, displaying a strong, if slightly puerile, sense of humour. Our laughter, shared by Sara, seemed both to surprise and encourage him. Further social encounters over the following weeks drew him still further out of his shell until, within our small circle at least, he came to adopt the court jester's role we all enjoyed.

But it was only with time, that we came to realise how we had initially mis-read the situation, and that the truth slowly began to emerge.

Rupert's real name, it transpired, was actually Brian. To Sara, he had always been Rupert from childhood, so it was natural that we should use the same name.

It seems that Rupert, or rather Brian, had been orphaned at an early age when his parents died in a car accident, whilst on overseas service in Africa. His childhood was spent in the care of several aunts, of whom his favourite was a near neighbour and friend of Sara's mother. When Sara and brother Tim were home for the holidays, Rupert would be a frequent visitor, and eventually became a regular house-guest. Sara often spoke of the games they would play in the vicarage garden and surrounding fields during the long, hot summers, and of the special occasions when the three were allowed to sleep out in the tent.

It must have been during that happy childhood that Brian acquired the name of Rupert. Both Sara and Tim were ardent fans of the famous bear and the three would re-enact his adventures, with the part of Rupert being given to Brian. He entered into the spirit of the game and his allotted role to such an extent that, with time, he even unwittingly came to acquire some of the mannerisms of their hero. Physically, he already bore some resemblance, being rather short, slightly plump, and blessed with a fair, clear complexion and a head of tightly curled, blond hair. I swear that his dress, even today, is modelled on that of the original Rupert. Only on the very hottest of days, for example, would he abandon the long woollen scarf, which had become his trademark. His use of 'Boys Own' language too started as part of the game, was perpetuated as a joke, and accounts for his frequent use of outdated expletives and clichés, even today.

Rupert's educational achievements, or non-achievements, were something I never delved into - these had no bearing on our relationship. Suffice it to say, that he possessed the quick wit of the jester but no great depth of intellect. In our small group, therefore, he was well qualified for his adopted role, and on occasions his willingness to ingratiate himself with us was cruelly exploited. He was clearly driven by a strong need to belong to our small circle, possibly as a consequence of the rootlessness of his own upbringing. It would be an exaggeration to say he clung to Sara - but he was certainly very supportive, even to the point of servility.

All this we established in the course of various contacts with the two of them, as well as in midnight conversations with Sara, tongues loosened by a glass of wine. Whilst the pieces of the jigsaw were fitting together, the question of Sara's personal relationship with Rupert remained unanswered and became the subject of frequent conjecture. Until that first night at the cottage, I was convinced that there was no sexual bond between them - that Rupert was more a convenience, which Sara wouldn't allow to stand in her way if she were to meet someone else. In other words, he was no more than the cuddly bear she had always known, and a comforter to help her through life. Perhaps the sexual side of their relationship was to be viewed in the same light.

2

Rupert had been right about the weather - brass monkey's, he had called it. It had turned progressively colder as the Friday approached and there was even a suggestion of sleet in the rain, as Beck and I sat in the rush-hour traffic on Western Avenue. The occasion was a hen weekend, our destination, a cottage on the edge of the Cotswolds. The hen weekend itself was really just a pretext for the four of us, Beck and I, Sara and Rupert, to meet up and enjoy ourselves - the official hen party was due to take place at a tapas bar in two weeks time, when a whole crowd was expected.

Beck's wedding had been planned for some time. It was just the idea of the weekend away which was born on the spur of the moment - in the Greasy Spoon, in fact, after a hard session on the river - and it went without saying that Rupert would have to be a hen for the purposes of our plans. He and Sara seemed inseparable, apart from which his ready wit was always a welcome addition to any party.

The practical arrangements had largely been left to myself and Beck. The renting of the cottage was the easiest part, the logistics proved more complicated. Despite an impressive collection of degrees between us, the planning of detail was not our forté. Nevertheless, it was finally arranged that I would take my car, meeting Beck from work, and together picking up Sara from Cheltenham station, where she would arrive off the Reading train. Travelling down from Manchester, Rupert would join us at the cottage.

January was not the ideal month for our little adventure, and neither was it the best time of the year for a wedding. But planning considerations rarely apply to affairs of the heart, and the fact of her pregnancy had only served to confirm Beck's decision to marry Tony and to hasten the wedding. For his part, Tony had had his sights set on marriage from the outset and looked on Beck's pregnancy as providential.

The traffic had finally begun to thin, as we crossed the Chilterns on the M 40. The sleet had now turned to wet snow and heavy flakes hurled themselves at our headlights, as if hell-bent on self-destruction. The rhythmic motion of the windscreen wipers began to make me drowsy and, just when I most needed her company, Beck had chosen this moment to go to sleep. I put a tape in the cassette player and the up-lifting tones of Vivaldi filled the car, but not so loudly as to disturb my sleeping passenger. It wasn't a bad stereo at all for a small 1300 hatchback. That was one benefit of the job at U. I. Foods.

The train arrived twenty minutes late at Cheltenham, an occasion for profuse apologies over the P.A. system. Being late ourselves, we arrived just as the train approached the station. Coming straight from a new product launch for a client near Reading, there had been insufficient time for Sara to change out of her work clothes. She was wearing a calf-length, navy-blue coat, opened down the front to provide glimpses of long legs under a short, tight skirt and buttoned jacket. As always, heads turned at the sight of this blond apparition, high heels clacking over the wet platform, as we rushed forward to take her briefcase and overnight bag.

"Greetings peasants!" came a voice from the hall.

"Rupert!" we cried in unison, crowding round, for a kiss and a hug, for all the world like adoring nieces, welcoming their favourite grown-up uncle.

"Nice pad," said Rupert, looking round approvingly.

The cottage was, indeed, quite delightful. Standing in the grounds of Overton Hall, it was one of a pair of early, converted workmen's cottages. Off the entrance hall to the right, there was a sitting room with a small dining room opposite, which in turn opened on to a lean-to kitchen at the back. The first floor comprised of two small bedrooms, together with a tiny bathroom. Beck and I were to share one room, Sara and Rupert the other.

As it was already quite late, we decided to eat at

the Crown and Trumpet in the village. The pub was pleasantly crowded with a cross-section of the local community and, despite being the only 'foreigners', our presence attracted little interest. We ate well and unhealthily.

The conversation over our meal ranged far and wide, but was largely inconsequential. It struck me that Rupert was quieter than usual. From experience, I knew that he felt happier in some situations than in others - he was at his best, for example, when accompanying the television with a stream of witty, and sometimes quite perceptive, remarks. As the talk increasingly turned to rowing matters and acquaintances, Beck, with her more highly developed social sense, intervened to draw him into the conversation.

"So what took you off to sunny Manchester then, Rupert?" spoken with one of her winning smiles. "Bit off your normal beat, isn't it?"

"Oh, you know," said Rupert, shifting slightly on his seat, "few problems to sort out. Spot of 'trubble at t'mill', as you might say. Board not too happy with the way things were going there. A lot of my key accounts are handled from the Manchester office, you see, so they sent me up to sort things out, kick ass, as they say."

Rupert, I should explain, was a senior account manager in a large market research organisation.

"And did you find any ass to kick, or whatever?" asked Beck with mock innocence.

"Cheeky!" said Rupert, giving Beck a hearty shove that nearly landed her on the floor. But her intervention did the trick and he soon had us in fits, before we spilled out into the night, at closing time.

The sky had cleared and the temperature dropped still further and, although it was only a short walk back to the cottage, we felt thoroughly chilled by the time we got there. Too late to light the fire, we sat huddled in the kitchen over hot chocolate, and discussed plans for the next day. Beck and I would go on a girlie shopping expedition to Cheltenham, (Rupert's choice of words, not mine), at the same time buying the provisions for my special dinner in the evening. Sara and Rupert were to visit Sara's mother in Herefordshire.

The next day dawned bright, crisp and clear. It was only then, that we were able to appreciate fully the beauty of our surroundings. Built of honey-coloured Cotswold stone, the Hall and cottages glowed warmly in the early-morning sun. Immediately behind the village rose the slopes of Bredon Hill. The green of the grass was tinged with frost, and the sheep, dotted over the hillside, looked like cream-coloured blobs, as if painted by a child.

Beck and I had been back from Cheltenham about two hours before Sara and Rupert returned. By their standards, they were relatively subdued, even dejected, and it was not until after the second glass of champagne that they recovered sufficiently to talk about their visit to Sara's mother.

Gloria now lived alone in what, for thirty-five years, had been the family home. This was a rambling, Victorian vicarage, standing in its own grounds in the village of Great Langford, some fifteen miles from Hereford. The house had been bought with family money following the death of Sara's paternal grandparents, who had owned rubber plantations in Malaya. Sara heard little from her father these days, and saw even less of him. It seems that he had taken off, some years ago, with what Sara called his bit of stuff. In the settlement Mummy had received the house, a lump sum, which she had quickly squandered, and a nominal annuity. The house, although in need of some renovation, undoubtedly represented a significant asset, particularly in view of the outline planning permission to build up to ten houses on part of the land.

What had particularly upset Sara was Mummy herself. In her youth, Gloria had been an aspiring actress but, even in her prime, had never risen above occasional bit parts, and many of these had been in less than memorable commercials.

According to Rupert, Sara had inherited her good looks from the maternal side but they both felt it would be kindness indeed to describe Gloria, now, as even a faded beauty. She had seemingly aged beyond her years, thanks in part to her earlier zest for life, but more directly to the ravages of alcohol and tobacco. Always a flamboyant figure, she now looked little short of bizarre, the dyed jet black of her thinning hair and eyebrows standing in stark contrast to the visibly sagging skin of her neck and upper chest. The vivid red Cupid's bow lips rounded off an almost ludicrous appearance.

Genuine concern, however, now overlay Sara's embarrassment when talking of her mother. It seems that both she and Rupert suspected her of showing early signs of Alzheimer's Disease. Like many alcoholics, Gloria had learned over the years to compensate for the impairment to her faculties, brought about by prolonged drinking. Now, either her intake had increased or, with the onset of years, she was no longer able to cover up so successfully for her habit. Either way, her behaviour had apparently become even more eccentric and her motor reactions less controlled. Sara dreaded to think what would happen if, or rather when, her mother was no longer able to care for herself. One thing was sure - there would be no help forthcoming from brother Tim. Whilst sympathising with Sara, we were certainly not going to let Gloria spoil our evening - after all, this was Beck's hen party.

My dinner was a great success, thanks in no small measure to Delia Smith and copious quantities of wine, followed by port and, later still, brandy. An unruly game of Scrabble led to a dispute over the validity of a number of highly questionable words. With no dictionary and no neutral adjudicator to refer to, the game had to be abandoned without a winner. Rupert suggested something less cerebral, so we trekked across the yard to the Annexe.

The Annexe was an agricultural outbuilding, converted into a games room for the benefit of holiday guests. It was so cold inside you could see your breath, calling for an energetic session of table tennis. A game of Round the Table was followed by a seriously competitive game of doubles. Beck and I won the first game, but the match abruptly terminated when Rupert accidentally trod on the only ball. We then launched into a ferocious game of darts, 501 being followed by Round the Board and finally Cricket. By this time, more darts were missing the board than hitting it. A classic case of games fatigue, it was decided. Clearly, there was only one thing to do! Back to the cottage to stoke up the fire and crack open another bottle.

It was nearly two o'clock before we finally dragged ourselves off to bed. The sheets felt icy and, despite the combined effects of fatigue and alcoholic stupor, it was some time before I warmed up sufficiently to drop off. Before reaching this happy state, we heard raised voices from Rupert and Sara's room. Beck and I looked at each other across the gap between the beds, and shrugged shoulders under the bedclothes. Later still, I was dragged back into semi-consciousness by the unmistakable sounds of love-making from the next room. Turning over, I pulled the bedclothes tightly round my head and slept soundly till first light.

The next morning, the day of the pony trek on Bredon Hill, was to be the high point of the weekend. The lovers came down late for breakfast and exchanged hardly a word. If I were superstitious, I might already have recognised certain signs, portents, of what was to come: the dead bat lying in the yard outside; the elderly lady who had collapsed, the previous day, in the shoe department of Cavendish House in Cheltenham; the wine spilt over dinner and running onto the floor like blood; even the love-making, like the condemned man's last meal - all these meant nothing to me at the time but, with hindsight, may have held some special, unrecognised significance. Rupert and Sara's mood at breakfast might be added to this list. But in practice, nothing could have prepared us for the sheer, numbing horror of what actually happened.

The stables were only a short walk from the holiday cottage. There, 'Old' Mr. Rogers introduced us to the ponies. Beck and I were allocated the two most docile beasts, Dolly and Madge, who knew their way round the hill blindfold - or so it was claimed. My experience of horse-riding is only limited and I felt apprehensive, as did Beck. Rupert and Sara, on the other hand, had often ridden as children and didn't share our misgivings. We were made to ride ahead, with them bringing up the rear.

The first part of the ride was a gentle ascent along a stony bridle path, and called for little concentration. As the houses dropped away behind, the cold morning air brought welcome relief to my head, clearing the effects of the previous night's alcohol.

What caused Sara's horse to bolt, no-one afterwards could say. A sudden commotion behind had broken into my thoughts but, before I could turn round, I was passed by Sara, desperately trying to control her horse. The crazed animal had taken a narrow sheep track, striking off at a tangent down the side of the hill at a lower level. Its doomed charge brought it only fifty yards before it slipped and crashed onto its side, rolling over once, before coming to rest in some low scrub. Motionless, its back broken, only the wild, terrified stare of its eyes betrayed any vestige of life. With one foot still caught in the stirrup, Sara lay on her back, pinned beneath the creature, the life seemingly crushed out of her. Her face was grey, the eyes open, unblinking, showing only the whites. With great presence of mind, Beck jumped down from her horse and scrambled over to where rider and horse lay. Remembering her first-aid training and the need to ensure a clear airway, she bravely attempted to open Sara's jaw but screamed and recoiled in horror as the blood welled up out of the corner of her mouth. Sara was dead.

I always used to be a happy sort of chappie, until I landed up here. Some might say I was shallow, too flip, but I'd say to them: "You don't know me!" You have to really know me to *really* know, if you get my meaning. I can see that now - now I've got time to think about these things, ponder on life, as it were.

I suppose the happiest time of my life was when we were kids, Sara, Tim and me. Africa is largely a blank, my Early African Period, I call it, but I don't let on. I can picture my mother though. She was pretty with a lovely smile and always smelt nice when I pressed up against her. I can still smell her now if I really concentrate. My favourite time was when Daddy was away up country and I was allowed to get into bed with her. Sometimes I would dream that Daddy was dead and I'd be glad because it meant I could share Mummy's bed forever.

Daddy was tall, lean and bronzed with thick curly dark hair and a beard tinged with grey. He always wore a bush hat and dark glasses, possibly, as I now realise, to hide his lazy eye. This gave him a wild look, sort of mad, which frightened me.

We got up to some great pranks, Sara, Tim and me. I remember the time I stole a tube of Smarties from the shop as a dare. Sara acted as decoy - she could charm the pants off anybody with her curly blond hair, blue eyes and little-girl lisp. She said I was her hero, her champ, so I let her share them and we ate them all at one go. The empty tube we put in the waste bin by the school gate - hid the evidence, see. Clever, what?

And then there were the dens. Our favourite was on the bank of the brook, sort of inside a huge bush and pretty well hidden. That was where we thought up most of our super wheezes. The earth was bare and packed down and always gave off a funny smell. The only drawback was the flies which reckoned it was their home as well. There was a low branch you could sit on, polished from use. Sometimes this would be a bench when we played 'school'. By balancing an old plank across to another branch, it became our dining table when 'dinner was served'. Or the examination table when we played doctors and nurses. In the hot summer, you had to take your clothes off to play a lot of the games and if you were naughty you were spanked. We got into trouble with Auntie Gloria once when Sara split and showed her the red weals on her bottom. But it was pretty innocent stuff really - it didn't get rude till later.

There was one occasion though when things did get a bit out of hand. We'd seen some film on TV, an old black and white movie, where this barn went up in smoke and people rushed about with buckets of water, shouting. It was Tim's idea to re-enact the film but on a smaller scale. I thought it was a spiffing idea and it was me who started the blaze. How was I to know that the blasted wind would get up just at that moment? Anyway, our attempts at putting it out were useless and there was nothing we could do but get the blazes out of there. That's a pun, ha, ha. They never found out how the fire started. The favourite theory was that it was ignited by the sun, beaming through a broken bottle. Everything was tinder-dry at the time. I told Auntie Mary this was almost certainly the cause. After all, I could speak from experience - you can fry ants through a magnifying glass. Did you know that? I hate ants - they're vicious little bastards.

3

The coroner's verdict was one of death by misadventure. Gloria, it appeared, had filled the kettle, turned on the gas and gone in search of matches. By the time she returned, some time later, a high concentration of near-odourless gas had built up in the kitchen. Had she remembered why she left the kitchen in the first place, and attempted to light the cooker, there would have been a fatal explosion. As it was, she pottered about preparing the tea things until, unaware of the danger, she succumbed to the lethal fumes. The local police found her collapsed on the floor when they came to break the news of Sara's death. Their attempts at resuscitating her were unsuccessful.

Presumably out of consideration for the family, no direct reference was made by the coroner to Gloria's known attachment to drink, although a high concentration of alcohol was found in her blood together with traces of a number of drugs. These had apparently been prescribed by her GP whom, unknown to Sara, she had been seeing about her ailments. Whilst these facts were recorded, they were not considered to be a major contributory factor in the tragedy, and the inquest was conducted very much as a formality. Nevertheless, the national tabloids managed to get hold of the story. Headlines such as 'Double Death Mystery' and 'Mother and Daughter Death Riddle' ran for several days as every possible theory for the coincidental deaths was explored and exploited. It was even suggested that Gloria possessed extra-sensory powers, and took her own life in telepathic response to her only daughter's death. None of these so-called investigations added anything to the coroner's own findings or achieved much, other than to boost readership levels. The local paper took the opportunity to run a supposed horse-riding safety campaign, highlighting the surprising number of fatal riding accidents, which had occurred in the county over recent years. In reality, this was only a pretext to recycle old news of the more sensationalist kind and, for the general public, the tragic events of that weekend faded into obscurity within a matter of days. For Beck and myself, the horror and implications of those events grew like a cancer day by day, and night by night.

The funeral was an ordeal. Although a double one, it was for me Sara's funeral; after all, I had never met Gloria. I cannot claim to have much experience of funerals but I have been to a few. As a non-believer and infrequent churchgoer, the service itself usually leaves me feeling detached, if not cynical. Maybe that's because the deceased had, until now, more or less achieved their full life span. Their death had been a natural event, and the funeral was the socially accepted way of saying goodbye. In Sara's case, her death was premature and unquestionably tragic. All the clergyman's trite-sounding clichés, which would normally have produced in me a mental sneer, struck a definite chord - and not just in me alone. Rupert and Tim were inconsolable in their grief, which was shared in considerable measure by all the mourners who had known Sara personally.

It was the first time I had been to the Old Vicarage. It was a house built to be filled with sunlight and children but today it felt damp, cold and cheerless and I was sure I could smell the remains of the poisonous gas, which had killed Gloria. It seemed wrong to be meeting in a place where, just a few days earlier, someone had died.

Only now, at the reception, was it possible to see who was who. Many of the mourners at the church had clearly been people from the village who had attended the service out of idle curiosity. Here at the house, the gathering was sparse, the mood sombre. The good ladies of the church, which Gloria had apparently not patronised, did their best, providing tea and sandwiches with British sherry served to those requiring 'something stronger'. The undertaker, also invited, never took off his black raincoat. That summed it up for me.

For whatever reason, Sara's father's side of the family was not represented. A deliberate snub? Who could tell. In Gloria's case, there were literally no immediate relatives to invite. Her own parents were, of course, long since dead as would have been any uncles or aunts. An only child herself, that left just Sara and Tim.

We had had to rely on Tim to notify those of Sara's friends with whom we were not in regular contact - former school friends and some of her Oxford chums whom we didn't know. Few of these were present and I wondered whether the news had even reached them. It seemed odd that Sara and Tim had drifted apart since leaving home and moving to London - in childhood they had, after all, been very close.

For Beck and I, the grieving process didn't end with the funeral. On returning to my place, we both felt so totally drained that it seemed the most natural thing in the world to climb, exhausted, into bed and pass a restless night clinging onto each other.

The atmosphere at the official hen party too, as well as at the wedding itself, was muted but, despite everything, both took place as planned. The wedding, however, wasn't the great society occasion Beck's parents had wished for. In the event, it was something of a hole-in-the-wall affair, despite the fact that it was held at Chelsea Register Office. Only a handful of immediate friends and relatives attended, and there was neither a grand reception nor luxurious honeymoon. After the ceremony, the party moved on to the nearby Man in the Moon, the honeymoon couple leaving later for a long weekend in the West Country where it rained non-stop. Not a very auspicious start - not that that had any bearing on later events.

The marriage broke down in a matter of months - poor Beck was devastated at the time. The first problem was the miscarriage. Whether this was in any way connected with the accident on Bredon Hill, it was impossible to say, but the events of that weekend certainly couldn't have helped. At first, it looked as though Beck and Tony's marriage would survive this crisis but it soon became apparent that, without the baby, there was little to hold them together. Also, given the seeming security and intimacy of the married state, Tony saw fit to exercise some strange sexual practices which Beck found quite distasteful.

Tony had been married before. I don't know how much Beck knew of the circumstances of this marriage and the cause of the break-up. At that stage, she was understandably loyal to Tony - Melanie had been a 'cow', and Tony had been lucky to get out of it as cheaply and painlessly as he had. Thank God there were no children.

The whole episode left her more disillusioned than bitter - or maybe it was just a stage in the psychological healing process. But two major traumas in the space of just a few months......

For my part, I was glad to have Beck back. I'd got used to having her around and had found it difficult to adjust to being on my own again, which is possibly why I had so readily put out the

'Welcome' mat for Randy.

Randy was a mistake. A drifting American, he had hung around on the fringes of our group, striking up relationships as, and wherever, he could. As an exchange student, he had enjoyed life in England so much that he opted out of his studies and stayed, or should I say, stuck.

It was his attractive voice and sense of humour, which I fell for - he could also be quite charming. He was between flats at the time I met him and was more than ready to accept a roof over his head and to share my bed. Financially, he contributed nothing to the household, on the contrary. As well as being between flats, Randy seemed to be permanently between jobs, and it was Beck's return, which finally provided me with the excuse to give him the heave-ho. Randy's randiness, at first a novelty, was not missed, which is more than could be said for some of my more valuable possessions. Perhaps he just wanted a keepsake to remember me by.

Beck's return brought an element of stability into our lives and allowed us to pick up the threads of our social life, where the first priority had to be to run Rupert to ground. We had both tried independently to get hold of him, without success, and felt hurt that he, for his part, had made no attempt to contact us. Surely he couldn't feel we had only accepted him as an adjunct to Sara, not as a friend in his own right.

No-one answered the first couple of times we rang the flat. On the third occasion, a stranger picked up the phone. He didn't know any Rupert, or

Brian for that matter. I checked the address - yes, that tallied. Perhaps our friend had been a previous tenant - they had only moved in three weeks ago themselves. I was given the name of the estate agent who handled the property. Maybe they could help me with a forwarding address, meanwhile, if I fancied meeting for a drink.......

The best course of action, we decided, was to visit the estate agent in person. With hindsight, the same result could have been achieved with a phone call, saving the journey to the Edgware Road. All we learned there was that Mr. Cunningham had indeed moved out. He had sacrificed a sizeable slice of his deposit in lieu of notice, and all outstanding accounts had been settled. Rupert had not left a forwarding address and the agent would not have been at liberty to give it to us had there been one. Mr. Cunningham had handled matters himself. No, there had been no solicitor involved.

We felt both hurt and sad that Rupert had apparently walked away from us in this way.

It must have been around this time that Irena, briefly, came into our lives. Newly arrived from her native Romania, she had acquired a job in Beck's office as a junior researcher in the East European section. Generous by nature, Beck must have shown her some small kindness as a newcomer, which was enough for poor Irena to become a friend for life. To Beck, she was like a puppy dog, which couldn't leave her side or, more cynically, like a parasite on its host.

I'd always felt there was something strange about her and it wasn't just her appearance, although this was odd enough. She cut a diminutive figure and as far as dress went she was locked in a '70's time warp. But what she lacked in stature, she certainly made up for in strength of will. Even Beck, who is more tolerant than I, found her overbearing and could only take her in small doses.

I clearly remember the first time she came round, and the instant dislike I took to her. It was a Friday night and I had been looking forward to the weekend. What may have passed in her own country for conversation bordered, by our standards, on interrogation. It's quite flattering in a way for someone to take an interest in you but I didn't want to be cross-examined, neither did I want to learn all about our guest herself. Having completed her studies in her native Craiova, she had lit upon the idea of coming to England for a year to improve her English which, I grudgingly have to allow, was excellent. Through a contact of her mother's at the British Council in Bucharest, she had succeeded in securing the temporary post at the BBC where, according to Beck, she was rapidly driving everybody mad.

I suppose I was more annoyed with myself than with Irena, annoyed, that is, for allowing her to expose my emotions so easily. Before I knew it, she had me talking about Sara and the dreadful accident. Irena lapped it up, sitting on the edge of her chair and leaning towards me with the sympathetic air of a counsellor, relishing every moment.

She explained how her mother, in her day, had been a famous medium and helped a number of prominent members of the political hierarchy. Although Irena herself had never practised, she had attended some of her mother's sessions and inevitably acquired some of her knowledge. Unlike her mother though, she laid no claims to any special powers but could record one or two 'experiences', and liked to read books on the paranormal. As Sara had not long been buried, Irena felt we should try to reach her through a seance. She had never actually held one with herself acting as the medium but knew exactly what to do. Beck didn't express an opinion, but I thought the idea ludicrous and lost no time in saying so. My opinion, however, cut no ice with Irena whose determination to press ahead grew even stronger with each objection. Without either of us having agreed to anything, Irena eventually left, promising to arrange everything for Sunday night.

Despite my scepticism, I couldn't help feeling a little nervous as the appointed hour grew nearer. I had even tried to persuade Beck to phone Irena and put the whole thing off, but she was prepared to keep an open mind on the subject, which she claimed to find mildly amusing.

Before we were mentally and physically prepared, the door-bell rang to reveal a diminutive figure clutching a small, utilitarian suitcase and followed by a black-cab driver bearing a polished wooden table.

"Hi Irena! So nice to see you," smiled Beck, the perfect hostess, stooping to exchange kisses on both cheeks followed by a third one for good measure. I'd never seen her do this with anyone else before, male or female. Irena stepped forward, clearly about to perform the same ritual with me. Anticipating the move, I too stepped forward, but proffering an outstretched hand, at the same time half-leaning backwards. Surprisingly, she got the message - the English are so stiff and formal.

"We do provide furniture, you know," I joked feebly, trying to show that I was prepared to tolerate if not exactly like her.

"Ah, but it is most important to have a round table, Philippa, if your friend is going to come amongst us," she explained, with a serious frown.

"Yes, yes, of course," I said, trying not to let my irritation show.

"Also, I hope you are not expecting anyone else tonight," she said. "It is vital that there should be no more than three persons present." On this we were able to reassure her, though failing to grasp the significance.

It took some re-arranging of the furniture to accommodate the table with sufficient space for three chairs as well. From the suitcase, Irena produced three candles, a plastic sandwich box and a pack of partially frozen French rolls from Waitrose.

"We must create the right ambience, so the radiator should be turned up, and I need the rolls and *tocanita* heating up. She will be cold and hungry and must be made to feel welcome."

Irena read my puzzled look.

"*Tocanita*" is a Romanian dish. It's quite spicy

and will smell wonderful. I made it last night. But I need to know what Sara looks like, so I will recognise her. Sometimes several spirits come at once. So can you describe her to me, or better still show me a photo?"

We did both. The photo showed our crew proudly holding up their cups after winning at Ross-on-Wye. Beck and I had pride of place in the front row, clad in our unflattering, body-hugging Lycra kit. Sara in the second row was no more than a smiling face, but Irena seemed satisfied.

"Has your friend been dead very long?" Irena wanted to know. This was apparently important for the form of the seance. The answer seemed to be the right one. "It is always easier to make contact with those who have died recently, rather than at some time in the distant past, " she explained. Logical, I thought.

The curtains drawn and candles lit, the atmosphere in the room was stifling. The *tocanita* with the bread in the centre of the table really did smell most appetising.

"I want you to do exactly as I say," Irena briefed us, "and to focus all your thoughts on Sara. Shut everything else out of your minds. Also, we must be patient, very quiet and very patient. OK?"

Beck and I nodded in assent, the concentration mirrored in our faces. This is absolutely ridiculous, I thought.

"Now, hold hands to form a circle and we'll begin."

(Are you sitting comfortably?)

Irena leant back and closed her eyes. Beck and I exchanged glances. I couldn't read her thoughts.

"Our beloved Sara,....." Irena began. The remainder of her words were drowned by the thundering roar of a jumbo taking off from Heathrow. The noise seemed to last for minutes whilst Irena's lips silently moved.

(They don't normally come over so low. *'Thousands perish as pilot sacrifices own life in attempt to land holiday jet in Hyde Park.')*

"..........among us," Irena finished.

The incantation was repeated once more. The following pause seemingly lasted for ever. Beck suddenly shivered. Had it really gone cold? Did the candle flames really flicker or was it my imagination? I didn't imagine the gentle shaking of the table - after all, it was my knee that produced it.

"Sara, *draga*," Irena implored in her native tongue.

"Sorry, Irena," I interrupted, breaking the circle and standing up. "Sara no understand Romanian. Should've explained beforehand. My fault entirely."

"You *bitch*, Phil," Beck shouted. The normally level-headed Beck must have been going along with this mumbo-jumbo. Amazing.

"You are a stupid cow, Philippa. *Stupid, stupid cow*!" screamed Irena, walking over to the corner of the room where she stood with her back to us, stamping her foot like a spoilt child and muttering to herself in Romanian.

"Really, Phil," said Beck. "You could've made the effort."

"Sorry, just couldn't enter into the spirit of it."

"Very funny!"

It was some time before Irena turned round and rejoined us. We exchanged apologies, but both knew that they weren't sincere.

"We could try a different approach," pondered Irena after some time, "But it would mean visiting the grave."

This was soundly vetoed by both Beck and myself, after which the whole subject, thankfully, died a death, as it were.

Irena disappeared from our lives almost as quickly as she had come. Soon after the farcical seance, she announced her departure back to Romania where her mother had suffered a mild stroke and needed her help. The episode was never referred to again, Beck embarrassed over her gullibility and me over my crass behaviour.

It was the anniversary of Sara's death, which prompted us to revisit the scene of the accident.

Arriving about noon, we headed for the Crown and Trumpet and a leisurely lunch, after which we set about finding accommodation. Not having rooms himself, the landlord recommended Mrs Pomfrey at Home Farm, on the outskirts of the village, where we were offered a large double room with a view over the Hill. It was apparently unusual to have visitors so early in the year. The season normally started a little later with the Cheltenham Gold Cup week when all rooms in the area would be taken.

Mrs. P. was your archetypal farmer's wife, used

to spending a lot of time on her own whilst her menfolk were out working. This doubtless explained her readiness to gossip.

"So you young things are from the big City, then?" Mrs. P. rhetorically asked, confirming what she already knew. This was only by way of introduction to what she wanted to tell us.

"We had a party of young folk from London in the village last year - staying with Mrs. Anderson at the Manor. One got herself killed, out riding on the hill. It was shocking! They reckon it did for old Bill Rogers - it was him that hired out the horses. He ran the riding stables with George - that's his son. The judge tried to make out that the horse wasn't safe to ride and that they should never have gone out, with the ground frozen solid like it was. Load of nonsense, if you ask me, but he took it to heart. My Bill says it killed him, Bill Rogers that is. They have the same first name, you see."

In view of Mrs. P's comments, we decided to pay a call on George Rogers. I don't know quite what we expected from this meeting - possibly some element of mutual support. After all, we had each lost someone as a result of the accident.

George Rogers had actually been in The Crown and Trumpet the day before but we had failed to recognise him. If he'd recognised us, he certainly hadn't shown it. His attitude when we called was not exactly hostile, but neither was it particularly friendly. He was at a loss to understand what might have caused the accident and bitterly resented the coroner's implied criticism of his father. Bill had handled horses all his life and taught most of the youngsters in the area to ride. Ask anyone about Bill Rogers and horses - they'd tell you!

We asked whether Sara's horse might have been ill. Human beings, for example, are known to undergo temporary or permanent personality changes if they are suffering from certain illnesses - those that affect the brain, like a tumour, for instance. Had the horse been examined after the accident? Do they carry out autopsies on animals in cases like this?

George clearly resented our questions. The horse had been examined by the vet from Tewkesbury, before being sent to the knacker's yard in Gloucester. He'd found nothing wrong with her, nothing at all. Perhaps they should've examined the rider or, more to the point, that twerp with her. (Obviously George had been less than impressed with Rupert.) Yuppies down from London who don't know one end of a horse from t'other. They're the ones that should be looked at by a vet.

It was time to take our leave.

The compassionate visit to George Rogers had gone badly wrong and left a sour taste. We brooded over the conversation as we re-lived the events of twelve months earlier. Had everything possible been done to find out why the horse seemingly took it into her head to take off like a thing possessed? Did they follow the correct procedure in examining the creature before effectively destroying what might have been the evidence? Was George Rogers' attitude to our questions a purely emotional response, or was he trying to cover up for something? Not least, why had Rupert been unable to throw any light on the subject? After all, he had been riding alongside Sara - and where was he anyway? And what of Gloria's death? Had it really been a coincidence, a freak, or were the two deaths possibly linked after all? As we began the ascent of Bredon Hill, this time on foot, my thoughts dwelt on these questions and our last visit there.

In contrast to that visit, the weather now was unseasonably mild, with a threat of rain constantly in the strong west wind. At times, huge puddles stretched across the width of the path, and our jeans soon became caked with mud as water seeped through our inadequate footwear. Eventually, we reached the spot where Sara's horse had bolted, and slithered down the sheep track to the point where rider and horse had lain. The only visible signs of the tragedy were the tattered remains of a bouquet of flowers, still partially wrapped in the original cellophane. Who had left this pathetic tribute, we vaguely wondered. But before we could ponder on this or reflect further on the events of a year ago, a noisy group of mountain bike riders passed close by, interrupting our thoughts. The wind whipped up a fine spray of mud as the first drops of rain began to sting the face, signalling the time to terminate our visit to Bredon and head back to London.

In re-visiting the scene of the accident, we had not deliberately set out to look for clues, nor seek answers to unasked questions. As it transpired, the trip produced no clues and raised more questions than we could have imagined. It's not clear exactly at what point we decided to make it our mission to find out the truth about the accident but, by the time we arrived back in London that night, it had become a firm resolve.

It was now more vital than ever that we find Rupert. The question was, where to begin.

It was one of the high points of my life, the day they made me Rupert. It meant that every time we played the game, I automatically became the centre of attention, the leader. I was no longer an outsider, a boy from the village. They had to do what *I* said. And I wasn't going to let them down, so I threw myself into the role; I lived and breathed the part.

But with time, the novelty began to wear off for the others - I guess Tim resented the way I had taken over his position. Things came to a head one day when Tim refused point blank to play the game any more. So I hit him.

I'm not a violent person by nature, on the contrary. But I couldn't allow Tim to rob me of my status, least of all in front of Sara. So I hit him. The blood ran through his fingers as he turned and fled, clutching his nose.

I didn't dare show my face at the Vicarage for the next few days and when I did it was to return Lucky. Lucky was the family's pet golden Labrador. He must have strayed from the garden because when I found him he was locked in mortal combat with a notoriously aggressive fox terrier from the village. I managed to tear them apart calling on reserves of strength I didn't know I possessed. In the fight unlucky Lucky suffered a cut to the ear which bled steadily. He kept shaking his head to rid himself of the pain. The only problem was that this would spray blood up the walls of the Vicarage kitchen. Auntie Gloria was quite upset but rewarded me with a seat at the head of the table where I was served tea and cakes. My esteem was restored in Sara's eyes and Tim had to grudgingly concede defeat. There was no argument when I next suggested we play 'Rupert'.

I do like animals. I really do. I still don't know how I was able to cut poor Lucky's ear with my Swiss army knife. It wasn't like me.

4

Beck felt sure that the firm where Rupert worked was called Hamer or Harman something. A quick search on the Internet in her office produced the details of Hamer Industrial PLC, a conglomerate employing over 4000 with a string of operating companies, including Hamer Marketing Services. This had to be it! They even had an office in Manchester where Rupert had been working before the weekend of the accident.

Sheena in Human Resources couldn't have been more helpful but was unable to trace a Brian Cunningham in her records. She even searched back five years but without success. If our friend had been 'on contract', of course, he wouldn't show up on her computer. This possibility we couldn't rule out, but thought it unlikely - Rupert had always spoken as though it had been a steady job, that he'd been there for some years. Anyway, he couldn't possibly have held the post of Senior Account Manager as a contract worker.

"Is there another company in the Hamer Group, involved with market research?" we asked Sheena.

"Yes, there's H.M.R. itself. Sorry, Hamer Market

Research," came the reply.

So that was the answer, how stupid!

Could Sheena possibly give us the phone number?

She could actually do better than that and transfer us from her line, but it wouldn't do any good because she handled staff records for both companies, and her search had automatically taken in H.M.R as well.

So it was back to square one. It looked as though we would have to head west again, but this time to the village of Great Langford, the home of Rupert's aunt.

We had been introduced to Mrs. Carter briefly at the funeral, but had instantly forgotten her name and were not sure exactly where she lived. An enquiry at the village stores provided the information and it was an easy matter to find the house.

Number 11 Prospect Terrace was the end one of a row of former council houses on the edge of the village. As we walked up the concrete path, a small child, dummy in mouth, was wrestling with a rusting supermarket trolley in the garden next door. We suddenly had misgivings about the wisdom of our enterprise.

These were dispelled when Aunt Mary opened the door. She remembered who we were and made us comfortable in what she referred to as the parlour. Whilst she disappeared to make tea, we had time to take stock of our surroundings.

The parlour was a cheerless, cramped room,

overfilled with an odd assortment of furniture. The brocade-covered, three-piece suite was of indeterminate age, but the rogue spring which poked me in the groin had lost none of its youthful vigour. The top of the veneered chipboard coffee table had been lovingly polished, but this did nothing to hide the white stains and one of the black-lacquered, screw-in legs looked as though it might give way at any moment. On the mantle shelf stood a black-and-white photo of a smiling serviceman in uniform. But the photo which really attracted our attention was one of Rupert. This was clearly a school photo, in a cheap, silvery cardboard frame. Rupert, the object of our search, looked out at us self-consciously, his curly blond hair growing over his ears like a wig in the fashion of the time. We guessed his age at about seven.

Mrs. Carter put us right when she came in with the tea a few minutes later. Brian had been nine when that photo was taken at the village school. He'd been small for his age and most people made the same mistake. Her own boys had grown up and left home years ago and she missed not having them and Rupert around the place. She always enjoyed the company of young people and it was so kind of us to call and see her. We must promise to come again and meanwhile she hoped we'd call her Enid.

Enid! We thought we had been talking to Rupert's Aunt Mary. It looked as though we'd made some dreadful mistake!

Like her three-piece suite, Enid too was of indeterminate age. She could have been 50, equally she might have been 65. Her floral-patterned pinafore was stretched tightly over an ample figure and I was fascinated by a kind of wart on her cheek from which sprouted a tuft of wiry hairs. But she seemed a good soul at heart and, living alone, was more than ready for a good chat.

We explained how Rupert, or rather Brian, was a member of our little group and a dear friend. He had spoken often, and with affection, of his aunt in Great Langford who had brought him up, largely single-handed. But he had always referred to her as his Aunt Mary.

"Could there be another aunt, an Aunt Mary, at all? Perhaps somewhere else," Beck suggested, weakly. "We might have got it wrong."

"No! There's no-one else. You can be sure of that." Enid was so emphatic, even abrupt, that her denial barred any further discussion.

We tried to establish whether she heard regularly from Rupert and if she knew his present address. Surprisingly, Enid had not seen Brian since he left home at the age of sixteen - until the funeral, that is, and then she wasn't sure if he'd actually recognised her. He'd made no attempt to speak to her and she, in turn, had hesitated to approach him in front of his smart friends. She didn't have an address for him either - never much of a writer, it would have been something of a miracle if he had written to her.

Tell a lie! Enid did receive a post card from him. This came out of the blue, some time after the funeral, and she imagined Brian had gone on holiday, perhaps to get over everything. After some rummaging in a letter rack containing mostly bills, Enid produced a somewhat bent post card. The coloured picture was of a small child, dressed in traditional costume and holding a bunch of red roses. Overprinted in white script was the message, in English, 'Greetings from Spain'. The postmark over the stamp on the reverse was illegible and the message from Rupert gave nothing away - just the usual platitudes about the food, drink and weather. It was undated.

Enid gazed at the card with a wistful expression on her face. Having brought up Brian as her own, she clearly felt a strong affection for him, and his apparent selfishness in turning his back on her all those years ago must have hurt terribly at the time. But it was something which, with the passage of time, she had come to accept, and showed no bitterness or resentment now. We mustn't forget that Brian did have a very tragic childhood.

Eventually, the time came to leave - Beck had to catch the 7.10 BA flight to Amsterdam next morning for one of her regular jaunts. Aunt Enid insisted on kissing us goodbye, eliciting a promise to come and see her again soon.

Back in London, other problems awaited me - firstly, in the form of water dripping through the ceiling from the flat above and, secondly, in the guise of an invitation to a meeting at Head Office in two days time. A phone call to my guardian angel, Rich Tonks, confirmed that my life was yet again to be turned upside down. The details were filled in when I returned to my unhappy stamping ground, Milton Keynes.

U.I.F. was re-structuring, I was told, and merging two of its operations, which would mean an unavoidable element of rationalisation.

"Does that mean I'm being made redundant, Rich?" I asked, pointedly. After three years, I had finally managed to bring myself to call him Rich.

"Well," he replied, playing for time. "There will inevitably be some downsizing, you know, outplacing," he equivocated.

The purpose of calling me to Head Office, so Rich explained, was in case I should read about these changes in the press and to reassure me that my own position was secure. The fine detail had yet to be worked out, and they should be able to tell me something further within the next ten days. That was the good news.

The bad news duly followed, as promised, a week later when I was offered a transfer to the Birmingham office where I would handle a territory (that word again) incorporating Wolverhampton and the West Midlands.

No way, I thought, and, true to this sentiment, found myself a few days later without a job and, even worse, without wheels.

The lack of transport severely hampered our bear hunting activities, though in truth we were devoid of any ideas after the disappointing visit to Aunt Mary. In any case, my first priority was surely to find a job. The redundancy pay from U.I.F. was meagre and wouldn't last long, apart from which I really wanted to put the money towards an old banger to be shared with Beck.

As a stop-gap, I took a job in a local off-licence, only it was rather pretentiously called a wine cellar. The money came in handy but I lived in constant dread of being forced to empty the till at knife-, or worse still, gunpoint. The job columns, meanwhile, didn't hold much promise and it was at Beck's instigation that I eventually rang Sheena at Hamer's. She had been most helpful on the phone and Hamer was, after all, a big organisation.

Sheena remembered me and asked whether we had meanwhile managed to trace our friend. In response to my enquiry about work, she explained how any vacancies were first advertised internally, within the Group. As a consequence, relatively few appointments were made from outside. Hamers too, in common with many other large companies, was undergoing cutbacks and Sheena wasn't aware of anything suitable for me at present. The best option was to apply for a job as a researcher - these were fairly easy to come by - and use that as a springboard from which to pick up something better. She promised to send me an application form and arrange an interview with her supervisor, which she duly did.

It wasn't difficult to see why I was offered the job of researcher. The pay was a pittance and the work involved knocking on doors or standing in a draughty shopping precinct, clipboard in hand, whilst people scuttled by, eyes averted. Anyway, for better or for worse, I took it in the hope that the grass might nonetheless prove to be greener on the inside.

Only after I had been with Hamers a few weeks did it occur to me to make discreet enquiries to see if anyone there knew or had heard of Rupert, or even Brian, come to that. Opportunities were limited, as I generally spent only a couple of hours in the office each week, collating and filing my returns. No-one I asked had come across our Brian, which seemed incredible considering there was only a handful of people in our division enjoying the title of Senior Account Manager. One of the accountants, who was Nigel by day and Nigella by night, thought he knew a researcher answering my description, but didn't know his name and had never spoken to him - just admired him from afar. Anyway, the guy hadn't been in for some considerable time so, all in all, that didn't seem a very promising lead.

Having re-established myself as a contributor to the welfare state, my next priority was to organise some transport. Beck had offered to pay towards a car, but my own resources were limited and I didn't feel I could impose on her generosity and accept a disproportionately large share, not least when she herself didn't drive.

I felt guilty visiting my parents on two counts - firstly, because the trip was long overdue and secondly, because I hate begging, particularly now I am supposed to be a working girl of independent means.

It was a shock to see how much they had both

aged since my last visit, especially my father. The reason soon became apparent. A victim of the recession, he had been obliged to take early retirement and, whilst the severance package at first seemed attractive, it was clear they would not be able to enjoy the comfortable retirement they'd so looked forward to. They hadn't wanted to burden me with their silly troubles and Mum had come up trumps by helping for a few hours a week at the newsagents. My plan of asking for a loan in the hope that a gift might be forthcoming foundered - thankfully - before the subject could be broached. I slunk back to London, bowed by a double burden of guilt.

By going shares and stretching our resources to the limit, we were just able, with some haggling, to buy an ageing Citroen 2CV in an amazing combination of cream and pea green. Once I had sorted out the gears, such as they were, it successfully transported us from Hendon to Shepherds Bush, which was the last journey it managed without breaking down. To preserve our sanity, we convinced ourselves that the 2CV was a cult car and called it Nellie, because its top speed was about that of its elephantine namesake.

Would Nellie make it as far as Herefordshire, for that had to be our next move? We had drawn a blank in London and a further visit to Overton was unlikely to be productive. The only possible evidence from there had gone to the knacker's yard with the carcass and, even if the vet who had carried out the examination could be traced, we couldn't expect him to add anything to what was already in his report. The idea of questioning Bill Rogers again didn't hold much promise either, apart from which his underlying aggression could well turn to violence if he were put under pressure - he clearly harboured a deep resentment. A further visit to Enid in Great Langford had been promised but the chances of her having heard from Rupert in the meantime were a little remote. But there was another reason for making the trip West.

Visiting Bulstrode, Crabtree and Smith in Hereford was a long shot, but one worth taking. As family solicitor and executor, George Bulstrode had written for confirmation that we had no claims on Sara's estate. Presumably he had written to Rupert as well and might have, at least, a forwarding address. Rupert may even have been a beneficiary under the will.

George Bulstrode did not conform to the conventional perception of a solicitor, not even one from the country. He was a big man and breathing quite heavily by the time we reached the first floor and his office, which looked out over a jumble of rooftops, small back yards and an expanse of black, corrugated iron roofing. George looked as though he had just come from the cattle market. He was wearing heavy, brown brogues and green corduroy trousers, held up by a thick, leather belt. Instead of a pin-stripe waistcoat, a green quilted body warmer, open down the front, covered an open-neck chequered shirt. With powerful, raw-looking hands and ruddy complexion, George Bulstrode looked as though he spent most of his time outdoors, when not enjoying the good things of life.

This, it turned out, was almost the case. As a young man and only son, he had resisted parental pressure to work on the family farm and studied law instead. Now, with his father in his eighties and failing, George had stepped in to save the farm from 'the vultures', as he playfully put it. Most of the work in the practice he left to his partners but, as a family friend and erstwhile drinking partner of Sara's father, he had always looked after Gloria's affairs personally and, in so doing, sought to make amends for his friend's shabby behaviour.

I think that George took a shine to us or, more specifically, to Beck. After a cup of coffee in the office, we were invited to lunch at the Plough and Horses, round the corner, where he felt we could talk in more convivial surroundings. Although barely 12 o'clock, we readily agreed and, arriving at the pub, were shown to a quiet corner table where we continued what proved to be a fascinating conversation.

As is customary, George had written to all possible claimants on the estates of both Gloria and Sara. This had included ourselves as well as Rupert. The approach to Rupert elicited no response, and a recorded delivery letter was returned by the Post Office. The odd thing was that all Sara's personal possessions had been left in a pile of bin liners outside the Vicarage a few days after the funeral. These included all her private papers - even a small amount of cash - in fact, everything needed to execute the will. Only Rupert could have left these. Although George thought it was a damned strange way to carry on, he saw no reason to notify the police – after all, no crime had been committed.

"Whilst on the subject, are you girls aware of the terms of the wills?" he asked. "No? Then I'll tell you." This he proceeded to do.

Sara, on George's advice, had had a will drawn up some years ago and lodged at the practice. The terms were quite simple. If she pre-deceased Gloria, her estate would pass to her mother in its entirety and if Gloria pre-deceased Sara, the estate would pass to her brother, Tim. If she survived both, the beneficiaries would be a series of charities listed in the will. In point of fact, Sara's worldly assets amounted to only a few hundred pounds by the time her debts were paid off, which were not inconsiderable.

Gloria bequeathed a nominal sum to Mrs. Carter, her cleaner, with the balance to be shared equally between Sara and Tim. In the event of either pre-deceasing the other, the balance would pass to the survivor. If they both pre-deceased Gloria, then her estate, like Sara's, would be donated to a number of specified charities.

According to the medical reports, Sara had pre-deceased Gloria by about 30 minutes so that her estate, in a technical sense, passed in its entirety to Gloria. In practice, this didn't affect the outcome. With the exception of the nominal bequest to Mrs. Carter, Tim inherited the entire estates.

“Mrs. Carter?” I asked, “ Is that Mrs. Enid Carter from Great Langford, Gloria’s friend, Rupert’s aunt?”

This George confirmed, but pointed out that Mrs. C. was the lady who had come and done for Gloria.

“I wouldn’t call her a friend, as such. That would be stretching it a bit,” he felt.

I asked roughly how much the estate had amounted to.

“Hard to say, exactly,” was the reply. “The Old Vicarage and land represented the bulk of it. I valued the lot for probate at about £600,000. I’m told young Tim sold the land for development before putting the Vicarage on the market. Quite clever really. Some of the village elders not too pleased, of course. You know there was already planning permission in place for a number of houses. Started already, in fact. And the For Sale sign has gone from the house itself, so the deal must have gone through. I reckon Master Tim cleaned up quite nicely.”

This seemed a rather unprofessional thing to say but, as I said, George B. wasn’t your conventional solicitor.

“So, Tim has become quite a wealthy man - and a bachelor to boot,” mused Beck, stating the obvious.

“All depends how you look at it,” said George obliquely. A nerve close to his left eye began to twitch involuntarily.

It was also learned that all dealings with Tim had been conducted through a London solicitor. George could provide the address, if required.

We thought it was time to come clean, not that we had been deceitful towards George as such. With Sara and Rupert - sorry, Brian - we had been a close-knit group. Sara had died in a freak accident witnessed, apart from ourselves, only by Brian who, acting completely out of character, had seemingly disappeared. Gloria, Sara's mother, too, died in tragic circumstances. Brian's Aunt Mary turned out to be an Enid, Gloria's friend, disguised as a cleaner. And, relevant or not, the owner of the horse, or rather his son - because the owner's meanwhile died as well - turned aggressive when we started asking questions. It would be over-dramatising to say that something funny was going on, but George would understand why we were slowly becoming desperate to find Rupert - sorry, Brian.

Now on his second brandy, George did indeed understand but was unable, on the spur of the moment, to come up with any helpful suggestions. He would give it some thought, however, but meanwhile, if there was any other way in which he could be of *service....*, spoken with heavy emphasis, whilst fixing Beck with a watery stare.

It was nearer four than three o'clock when we finally poured out of the pub with our host. I didn't feel in a fit state to drive, apart from which Nellie wasn't allowed out after dark. (It was a miracle she had made it this far with only one hiccup and we didn't want to push either our luck or her.) Having already decided to put up for the night in Hereford, we told George we had some shopping to do, thanked him for his time and hospitality and said goodbye - he might have got the wrong idea if we'd asked him to recommend somewhere to stay.

The floor came up to meet me, and that is all I can remember until I regained consciousness, Beck's face framed by that hair hanging low over mine. She managed to get me onto the bed where I began to feel better after a cup of tea and a rest. Normally level-headed, Beck was shaken and insisted that we call a doctor, even though I had been out for less than a minute. This I emphatically refused, not wanting to make a fuss, but also frightened myself. Unknown to Beck, this was the second time I had blacked out, preceded in both cases by one of my headaches.

We were in a double room on the top floor of the mis-named Majestic Hotel by the station, a luxury I could scarcely afford on my pittance of a wage. But we had economised on the meal, a set Chinese for two. Walking back from the restaurant, any illusions of a peaceful market town had vanished as darkness fell and the night-life of Hereford swung into gear, heralded by the roar of engines and screech of tyres. We felt intimidated and crossed the road to avoid gangs of bellowing youths as they wove their way along the pavement. It made us feel prematurely old and vulnerable.

I saw things in a new light the next day, having recovered from my headache and refreshed by a night's sleep. It was a Sunday and too early to call on Enid, so it was decided first to visit the grave in Great Langford.

The grass in the churchyard had been freshly cut, leaving isolated the now fading clumps of daffodils. With an incongruously large, shiny headstone, Gloria and Sara's grave stood out amongst the older memorials to the dead of the village. 'Together in peace. Loved and sorely missed,' read the epitaph, along with dates of birth and the common date of death. I wondered, cynically, if Tim, for presumably it had been Tim, had chosen these trite sentiments from the funeral director's catalogue. The dead flowers in the cheap aluminium holder looked as though they had been left over from the funeral. These we replaced with our own humble offering, bought as an afterthought at the filling station on the outskirts of Hereford, throwing the old ones on a rubbish heap in the corner, piled high with grass cuttings.

A short walk down the lane brought us past The Old Vicarage. The new owners were clearly making up for the years of neglect and, despite the Sabbath, there was an odd assortment of white and red builders' vans outside. Scaffolding had been erected at the front, where one or two windows were broken. Down the side of the house, a new track, partly filled with hard core, had been cut by the wheels of contractors' vehicles, evidencing the start of building work on the new development. The rear garden had effectively been partitioned by a pale green, wooden fence, leaving the plot disproportionately small for the size of house. A sign at the entrance advertised luxury executive-style homes for the disserning (sic) by Dodge

Construction, to which a local wag had added a 'y', almost certainly not for the first time.

Not having a phone, we had been unable to check whether Enid would be at home and had only thought to drop her a line at the last moment. However, we were reassured to see her shadow approaching through the frosted glass of the front door. She had been unsure which day we were coming but had got in some nice boiled ham and hoped we would stay to lunch, which invitation we graciously accepted.

This time, we were ushered into the back room, which was cluttered but cosy. Enid clearly felt more at ease with us now and brought us instant coffee in mugs. I had problems handling the skin from the boiled milk, which clung to my upper lip and left me slurping over the drink like a geriatric. Beck developed an attack of the giggles.

It was too much to hope that Enid might have heard from Rupert again so soon and, sure enough, she hadn't. But she was more than happy to talk about his childhood and upbringing, during which some very interesting facts came to light.

"Were you related to Brian's mother or father?" we asked.

Mother, came the reply.

"And how old would Brian have been when his parents died?"

"Who said they're dead? *He* may be, for all I care, in fact I hope he is, but she certainly isn't and I can even tell you where she lives if you're interested."

"But Enid, Rupert's - sorry, Brian's - parents died in Africa, or that's what we were told."

"Africa? You'll be telling me next the moon's made of green cheese, I suppose," came the tart reply. "I'm sorry, I didn't mean to be rude. Perhaps I'd better tell you the truth. It can't do any harm now, can it? After all, I told Brian when he was fifteen. I thought he was old enough to take it - maybe that's why he went away," mused Aunt Enid and proceeded to pour out the secrets of Rupert's family history.

Enid was a good few years older than her sister, it seemed, and already married with two children of her own when Pat, at the age of fifteen, became pregnant. Although it wasn't a very posh neighbourhood, there was no way Pat could keep the baby - she was still at school, for heaven's sake. And so it was that Rupert, although never formally adopted, came to live with Enid and was brought up as one of her own.

Rupert's father, or alleged father, denied all responsibility and Pat admitted that she'd been sleeping around - you shouldn't say it of your own sister, but Pat was a tart, there was no way round it. They even suspected the same boy of being responsible for a later pregnancy, which was terminated.

Enid hadn't seen or spoken to her sister for years but produced the address with no difficulty. Brian too had been given Pat's address when first told about his parentage, and left to make contact, if he wished. Enid doubted if he had - it was all a long time ago now.

"So Brian made it all up - about his parents dying in an accident whilst on service in Africa?" We couldn't believe what we were hearing and needed confirmation.

"Well, that's a new one on me, but he was a fanciful child. I wouldn't go so far as to say he told lies, but he was always making up stories, you know, and play-acting. I used to tease him, call him The Great Pretender, like the song, you know. Oh, who was it by?"

Our perception of Rupert had clearly been wrong. To me, he had crossed the boundary between harmless fun, as Aunt Enid viewed it, and downright deceit.

"I think that was a bit before our time, I'm afraid. But tell me, how did Brian get on with your own two, Enid?" we asked. "Might he possibly have kept in touch with them?"

It seems they never really hit it off. Enid's own children had been that much older and quite independent, even at that age.

"But he was a lovely boy, most affectionate. The three of them - our Brian, Tim and little Sara - they made a lovely trio, you know. I can show you some photos, if you like."

From a bookcase Enid extracted a mock-leather bound album with 'My Family' embossed in gold script diagonally across the front, the viewing of which, with explanations and a break for lunch, took nearly two hours. We were shown sepias and faded brown photos of Enid's own parents and grandparents, as well as black-and-white pictures of her husband, the serviceman in the photo in the parlour. He had signed up as a regular after the war but was discharged on medical grounds. Jack had never been strong and died of pneumonia when the children were still small. One of the few photos of Enid and Pat showed two little girls squinting, white-faced, into the sun against the backdrop of a washing line.

Rupert was very prominent in the later pictures, popping up more often even than Enid's own boys. You could see why she had taken him to her heart. He really had been a very pretty baby and a delightful-looking child. Our own feelings towards Rupert the adult, however, were at that moment less than warm.

The last part of the album became more of a scrap-book, containing various cuttings about the children, swimming certificates and details of prizes won, along with some of Rupert's school reports. It was these which particularly attracted my attention.

It was clear that Rupert had worked his charm on the teachers too, even though they had to seek hard to find anything charitable to say about his academic ability. But what brought me up with a jolt was the name on top of each class report - Brian White. As long as we had known him, Brian's surname had always been Cunningham - to us he was Rupert Cunningham. Not only had he fabricated important details about his past, but now it seemed he had also assumed another name and an Aunt Mary to go with it.

"Did he change his name by deed poll?" we asked.

Enid wasn't quite sure what we meant. In bringing him up, she had always used the name White, which was Pat's name at the time and, of course, her own maiden name. Why ever should he want to change his name? We thought we knew the answer.

"What did Brian do after he left home? You said he went away when he was sixteen."

"I don't rightly know, my dears. He just said he'd got a job in Worcester, in a shop, and well, that was it really. I used to get the odd Christmas card, even a birthday card once. But he never came home again. I did miss him at first, you know, but my own are very good to me now."

The next few weeks provided little opportunity to reflect on our visit to Herefordshire, or discuss future strategy. For one thing, Beck had to make several visits abroad as well as attend a three-day conference in Edinburgh. At work, I at last got the breakthrough I had been hoping for in the form of a transfer to Client Liaison. It was just as well, as I don't think I could have carried on much longer as a clipboard girl. My new job involved preparing multi-media presentations for our senior executives. These were used mainly in negotiating for new business, but also in presenting the results of an assignment to the client. It was suggested that I would ultimately be heading up presentations such as this myself. I was thrilled. The salary was good, I would be off the streets, so to speak, and actually learning something new. Still no company car, but that might come later if I achieved sufficient seniority.

I'm not proud of what I did to Auntie Mary. In fact, if I'm honest about it, I guess I'm really rather ashamed. After all, she'd been very good to me, looking after me and everything. And it was wrong to take the money - it was the money she used to pay the electric and stuff. She kept it in the jam jars on the mantle shelf. And then to leave without saying goodbye or anything. She must have been well miffed. I thought nothing of it at the time. Later, I blamed it on the gang I got in with at the secondary school. Tim and Sara had gone away to boarding school then, you see, and I only saw them in the holidays. But that was just an excuse - I can see that now.

Worcester wasn't what it had been cracked up to be. In fact, life in the big city was a real bummer. No wizard wheezes in Worcester! Not even any Rupert games. But I kept the name, felt it set me apart, gave me a bit of class, do you know what I mean?

You need money to live, so you get a job, OK? Sounds easy, doesn't it? The first thing you have to do is fill out a form. I've never been any good with forms - it doesn't come naturally to a bear! And they want to know everything about you - and the rest. But the worst bit is the questions about qualifications. You see, I haven't got any - never passed an exam in my life. I never found out if it was best to lie or tell the truth. I tried both but it didn't seem to make any difference. Anyway, to cut a long story short, I finally got a job as an assistant in a department store. And Aunt Mary's money went on the deposit on my first suit. Made me look quite smart, although I say it myself.

Shop work doesn't pay very well, you know, and there's a limit to what you can fiddle. I had to do evening bar work as well, just to be able to pay the rent on my digs and the repayments on the suit. You're left with nothing for yourself at the end of the week.

But the worst bit was that in Worcester I was a nobody. And on top of that people either treat you like shit or shit on you, whichever. But the so-called suicide attempt was pretty pathetic. I can see that now. But then, it worked, didn't it?

You see, I had given Sara's name as my next of kin on the note. Just how obvious can you get? But the police managed to trace her to Exeter without giving the game away. She had just started her first year there. Next thing, there she was at my bedside at the Royal - though a basket of fruit is the last thing you need after being pumped out. But she re-kindled my fire and promised to find me a job in Exeter. So she could keep an eye on me, she said. So it worked out quite well after all, didn't it?

They're there again! The minute my back's turned they come crawling out. A whole bloody legion of them! But I will crush and destroy them. I will *stamp, stamp, stamp* them out!

5

Left to my own devices, I would never have got round to it. Beck knows what I'm like, which is why she took it on herself to make the appointment for me at the surgery. Dr. Singh gave me a fairly cursory check-up. My blood pressure was a bit high, for which he prescribed some pills, and told me to come back in a month.

"But what about the blackouts?" I asked.

"How many have you had?"

"Two," I replied. I had already told him this.

"Over what period?"

"About three months, I suppose. Not related to the time of month or anything, just out of the blue."

"Good," said Dr. Singh, although I don't know what was supposed to be good about it. "Let's get your blood pressure down first and then we'll see. Thank you."

I was dismissed.

The letter from George Bulstrode arrived a week after our meeting in Hereford. Rather pointedly, it was addressed to Beck.

Hereford

My dear Rebecca,

I very much enjoyed our meeting on Saturday and hope to see you here again before too long. I don't get up to London much these days but will certainly make a point of looking you up if I do. Meanwhile, I am enclosing the name and address of the solicitor handling young Tim's affairs in case you wish to contact him. You may also find the enclosed transcript of the sitting of the coroner's court of interest, although I don't suppose it contains anything you don't already know.

Respectfully yours,

George Bulstrode

On this last point, George was quite right, although it was interesting to see formal confirmation of what we had already picked up elsewhere. We couldn't get past the dragon of a secretary, though, when we tried to speak to Tim's solicitor on the phone. She was not at liberty to disclose personal details of any of their clients nor even confirm who their clients were. She could fit in an appointment in three weeks' time, if we wished to discuss the matter personally with Mr. Simpson, but was quite sure we would receive the same reply from him.

Getting hold of Tim wasn't that important in itself and it was rather half-heartedly that we wrote to him some weeks later, through Mr. Simpson, and in little expectation of a reply. As the weeks went by, it became clear that no reply would indeed be forthcoming.

Now armed with Brian's true name, I was able to make some progress in tracing him at Hamers. The news no longer came as a surprise that he had worked for the Company as a part-time interviewer, and had not reported in again since the day of the accident. Rupert Cunningham, Account Manager at Hamers Market Research, was a myth.

We buried Nellie in the June. I killed her; I readily admit it. Her brakes were never Nellie's best feature but that would be to make excuses. Call it a lapse in concentration or whatever, but it was an unequal contest from the start, a 2CV versus a Volvo V 90. A real David and Goliath situation, only in this case, David didn't win and Nellie has gone to that big scrap heap in the sky.

I burst into tears when it happened. The other driver was very nice, all things considered, and drove me home, clutching a pathetic assortment of belongings, salvaged from poor Nellie who I left by the roadside to be towed away. That was the reason why we had to take the train to Stockport rather than drive.

Visiting Rupert's mother really was a long shot,

but we were running out of options. The omens were not good. The introductory letter we wrote had been returned by the Post Office, marked ‘Gone Away’, with no further explanation. Also, the ticket clerk at Euston looked at us most strangely when we asked for an excursion to Stockport. When we arrived, our suspicions were confirmed - nobody had ever asked for one before.

Here, there was a keen wind to accompany the rain. In London, it had promised to be a really hot day and, stepping off the train, we felt distinctly underdressed. The source of the sickly smell on the wind was the brewery, the young Asian taxi driver explained to us. He seemed to find us fascinating and was quite charming, but his handsome face clouded over when we gave him the address. The reason became apparent as soon as we turned into the street.

The slates had been removed from most of the terrace, and grass grew up through the cobbles - called setts, as our guide knowledgeably informed us. The door of number 42 was hanging off its hinges, allowing a glimpse of débris in the room inside. ‘Gas off’ had been crudely painted on the door. The whole street was scheduled for demolition, we were told, and the residents had been re-housed, mostly in the old tower blocks in Brinkley. It wasn’t far, he would take us. Without waiting for an answer, he turned the car round and headed off. An enquiry at Chatterjee’s corner store provided Pat Robinson’s address on the sixth floor of Block C, and we handsomely tipped our handsome young driver before he sped away to look for another fare.

If I tell you that the lift didn't work, the staircase smelt of urine and the walls were covered in graffiti, I think you'll get the picture without the need for further graphic details. Things didn't get any better when the door to No. 614 was opened by Pat Robinson, née White, mother of Rupert Cunningham, alias Brian White.

Pat and her slob of a man took an instant dislike to us, and the feeling was mutual. She and her sister Enid were like chalk and cheese. Pat could well have been ten years younger than her big sister but, whereas Enid was large in a comfortable, homely way, fat Pat was just plain gross. On top of that, she insisted on wearing a tight, red, synthetic-leather mini-skirt which displayed her stockingless, blue-veined, cellulite-enriched thighs in all their glory. The tattooed boyfriend was equally overweight, casually clad in a pair of silky boxer shorts, out of which bits popped when he sat down, and a fetching little black, see-through top, providing a tantalising glimpse of nipple. We were there less than ten minutes in total, during which time, I'll swear, they smoked ten cigarettes each. With Pat for a mother, I could understand why Rupert had sought to create a new identity for himself. It was inconceivable that he would ever have wanted to acknowledge her existence, which is exactly how Pat acted in reverse. Even when shown the charming photos, which Enid had lent us, she simply denied any knowledge of

Rupert and rendered any further discussion pointless.

Our visit had turned out to be a complete waste of time, yet, from a feeling of anger towards him for having deceived us, our emotions after this meeting shifted slightly back in Rupert's favour.

The summer was exceptionally hot and, with little energy to spare, it was declared closed season for bears. I was becoming very involved with work, enjoying my new job which gave my life an added dimension. Beck had acquired a new admirer, of whom I didn't entirely approve. I have an innate suspicion of married men who claim to have an understanding with their wives, allowing each to pursue their separate 'interests'. And on top of all this, we tried to keep up our rowing. Perhaps it's not surprising, under the circumstances, that I completely forgot about my check-up with Dr. Singh. It was Black Saturday that brought matters to a head.

We had been invited to a party by a work colleague of Beck's. I felt decidedly provincial and out-of-place amongst this gaggle of screeching, boring, chinless wonders. With a drink in one hand and a chip on my shoulder, I accept that a combination of alcohol and attitude might have contributed to what happened.

Drama Queen was what Beck had called me. My fall down the stairs was certainly dramatic and put a definite damper on the evening. I remember commencing what was supposed to be a graceful descent after visiting the loo. Several million light years later, I came to, lying at the foot of the stairs with a second head growing out of the old one, and surrounded by a circle of concerned faces. My journey took me back to times and experiences I had not re-visited in an eternity. I was at a birthday party, Andrew Gregory's in fact, wearing a paper hat. Sitting opposite me at the dining table was my big brother, Mark, and Shirley Smith who had lived next door. The Smiths had emigrated to Australia when I was only five, and yet the vision of her, in my unconscious state, was as vivid as if the party had taken place only yesterday. The same applied when, minutes later, I lifted the table cloth to be quietly sick onto the floor after accepting a third helping of trifle. No-one noticed.

Other episodes from family history were re-enacted. The time when, picnicking on a holiday beach, a seagull scored a direct hit on Uncle Clive, and the occasion when my father, sitting in the garden drinking a cup of tea, gently sank to the ground without spilling a drop as the canvass deck-chair gave way. Childhood nightmares were also re-lived, as was the accident on Bredon Hill, with the difference this time that Sara got up and raised her knee sharply into Rupert's groin, whereupon he sank to the ground laughing uncontrollably.

Did I slip or was this another of my dreaded blackouts? Did she jump or was she pushed? Who can say. Certainly, mine host was taking no chances and, despite my protestations, insisted on calling an ambulance. My presence was clearly an embarrassment and this was the most effective way of despatching me.

A. and E. is not the place to visit on a Saturday night, unless you have masochistic tendencies, and I couldn't get out fast enough. In this, the patient and the nursing staff were at one. After being examined for concussion, I was packed off in a taxi and told to see my G.P. as soon as possible. Always one to procrastinate on matters medical, it wasn't until several days later that I visited Dr. Singh. The consultation was no more satisfactory than the first. He made light of my accident and only seemed interested in my blood pressure. This was normal and I was dismissed with a repeat prescription.

Hereford

My dearest Rebecca,

You may remember me mentioning that all poor Sara's belongings had been mysteriously left outside the vicarage following the accident. It occurred to me that you may like to go through them before they are disposed of and take anything of use for yourself by way of a keepsake. Not that I'm the best judge, but some of the clothing looks quite expensive. You would also be doing me a favour as they are currently occupying our office filing room and from experience it would be impossible to get any money for them towards the estate.

I have been meaning to come up to London for

some time and could bring the things in the Range Rover. How would Saturday week suit you? We could go out to dinner perhaps, and take in a show.

Please give me a ring.

Affectionately yours,

George

My dearest Rebecca squirmed on reading affectionate George's letter, and I revelled in her embarrassment. Beck was only prepared to agree to his visit on condition that I supported her in an innocent subterfuge. She, looking pale but beautiful, would plead an attack of the vapours, which, translated into today's terms, would be explained as a heavy period. The suitor's ardour would thus be quelled. That he would divert his attentions to me was highly unlikely and a situation that I could easily handle.

And so it was that George duly arrived with no less than 24 black plastic sacks containing all Sara's worldly possessions. Any designs he may have harboured on the object of his passions were duly dashed before they could be launched, and the poor man found himself back on the M40 with no more than a cup of coffee and a damp handshake as rewards for his efforts.

The plastic sacks themselves would probably still have been there today, but for the fact that they occupied the entire sitting room. Neither of us relished the prospect of sorting out Sara's belongings and we had to steel ourselves to make a start.

Why do people assume you might want to wear the clothes of a dead person, least of all someone you'd known closely? In this case, purely practical considerations ruled out any such thoughts. Whilst similar to Sara in height, my bulges are distributed awkwardly and Beck is blessed with those generous hips. Apart from anything else, Sara could look like a film star in clothes which, on us, would look laughable. She'd had style. So the bulk of the bags, including kitchen paraphernalia, could be despatched to Oxfam, leaving us to go through the remainder in more leisurely fashion.

I suppose we are all hoarders, to a greater or lesser degree, and most of our personal possessions, if subjected to public scrutiny, would look like so much junk. Sara's effects were no exception. Some of the objects were familiar from visits to the flat, but it was the trinkets, souvenirs, mementoes, and plain bits of rubbish that were both pathetic and poignant, the contents of drawers which would normally never see the light of day. The only way to handle this was to be brutal and rein in our emotions. The bulk of it was gratefully received by the local primary school for their summer fête and bazaar. This left the most difficult part, which you could loosely call paperwork and included books, letters, bills, photos and so on.

My natural instinct was, with the exception of the few books, to consign the whole lot to the bin but, on further reflection, decided first to check the contents - you couldn't be sure that George hadn't overlooked something. Beck violently disagreed, which led to the only row I can remember in our relationship. She accused me of showing a ghoulish interest in Sara's affairs and wanted no part in it. As a consequence, the two remaining sacks stood untouched in the corner of the sitting room for several weeks until one evening, without a word being spoken, Beck untied one and began to empty the contents onto the floor. I squatted down beside her and together we tackled the thankless task.

It's unlikely that Sara herself had been a great letter writer, but this didn't seem to have stopped others writing to her. Most of this one-way correspondence was in the form of holiday post cards which, in any event, do not demand a reply. Some, going back a number of years, were from Rupert, signing himself 'Cuddles'. The majority, in fact, were from men, but the names meant nothing to us. However, Sara had apparently written intermittently to her father, although this correspondence had seemingly died out some five years ago. At one point, she must have had a steamy affair with a 'D' - at least that was the inference behind his passionate letters. These bore no address and no dates and it didn't take much to deduce that 'D' was already married. Beck found this correspondence particularly distressing, as her own relationship with the philandering husband was grinding to its inevitable conclusion. I can't say I was sorry.

Sara's approach to bills seemed to be to stuff them into a drawer and hope they would go away. The fact that they did not was evidenced by the number of red final demands. To what extent Rupert managed the household accounts and eventually picked up the tab, it was impossible to say. We knew they had both kept separate bank accounts - a wise move on Rupert's part - and George must have retained the bank statements together with details of any investments. There were however stacks of credit card counterfoils, indicating that Sara had bought just about everything using a battery of different cards. It was amongst these that we came across several counterfoils, signed by Rupert against an Access card held in his own name. Of these, two in particular leapt out at us. One was for a meal bill for £62.50 from an Italian restaurant in Soho. Unremarkable in itself, except for the fact that it was dated *two days* before the fateful weekend in the Cotswolds - in other words, at a time when Rupert purported to be in Manchester! The second counterfoil bore the same date and had been issued by Eldorado Travel, London W1, value £180.00.

6

People of my parents' generation can remember exactly where they were, and what they were doing, when they heard of Kennedy's assassination. I was sitting at my desk at work, trying to unscramble a mess on my computer, when Uncle Clive rang. Dad had died of a massive stroke that morning. I felt the blood drain from my face and my knees went weak. It took some time to gather myself sufficiently and leave a message for my supervisor, before calling at the flat to pick up an overnight bag and head off to Nottingham.

Mum was in a terrible state when I arrived, and it only took one look at her for me to start blubbing too. It was only Clive's steadying presence which finally enabled us to pull ourselves together. I was grateful to him, just for being there, although he was clearly anxious to get back to his own family, now I was on the scene, and left at the first opportunity.

Next morning brought the arrival of Mark. I was relieved to see him and gave him a huge and tearful hug. But I was disappointed not to see his wife with him - I really liked Anne. It seemed that she and the kids would be down in a day or so, for the funeral.

Nowadays Mark and I only ever saw each other at rare family gatherings, but always got on famously. All the sibling jealousies of childhood had been filtered out with the years, leaving a deep affection. Like me, he had left home to go to college, never to return. Having achieved his qualifications in dentistry, he had joined a successful practice in York where he still worked and lived.

This meeting provided an occasion for fond reminiscences. We remembered, as teenagers, winding up poor Dad mercilessly when we felt he was being over-pompous, and how he had ridden our taunts and allowed himself, with good humour, to be gently deflated whilst preserving his authority as head of the family. Although the James' coffers had never overflowed, we had wanted for nothing, but equally had been made to work for luxuries and had never been spoilt. The bad times were forgotten, the good remembered.

Mark gently explained to me exactly what had happened to Dad. He had apparently collapsed straight after breakfast and never regained consciousness. He had died in hospital within an hour of admission. There had been nothing they could do to save him and, had he pulled through, he would almost certainly have been severely brain damaged.

The image of him lying on the dining room carpet - Mark had pointed out the exact spot - haunted me continuously through the next days, and even after the funeral. During that time, I proved an inadequate comforter to my poor mother - we had never been that close, I had always been Daddy's girl. Poor Dad, it seemed, had never really adjusted to being out of work after a lifetime of routine toil and I hadn't even known he'd lost his job. Prompted by an all-consuming guilt, I strove to be the model daughter as if in this way I could make up for the years of ingratitude and neglect.

I returned to London truly humbled and vowing to be a better person. Mum wanted to stay put amongst her friends, although she didn't rule out the possibility of moving into a small bungalow, once she had adjusted to her new circumstances. I promised to invite her down to London for a few days' sight-seeing and shopping, but we both knew the invitation would never be forthcoming and that, if it were, she wouldn't come.

London

Dear George,

I am so sorry I was unable to accept your kind invitation to lunch recently, particularly after you took so much trouble to bring Sara's things. I had been looking forward to it myself and hope you weren't too disappointed.

We finally managed to sort through the things and find homes for most of them. Amongst the papers, however, we did find some credit card counterfoils including one from Rupert which I am enclosing. I wonder if I could ask an enormous favour of you. I suspect that if we wrote to the travel company ourselves we would get a dusty reply, assuming they answered at all, but coming from you, a solicitor.....You see, the slip is dated just a few days before Sara's accident and we really do need to know what it was for.

I hesitate to ask this of you and wouldn't want to jeopardise our friendship by asking too much.

With all good wishes,

Rebecca

This letter cost no small effort and was the subject of many drafts. Beck initially refused to write it at all and only agreed under duress; after all, it was she who would have to fight off George's advances. But our search for Rupert had now become an obsession, and we desperately needed the answer to our question.

Hereford

My dearest Rebecca,

It was such a pleasant surprise to receive your letter and I am only too pleased if I can be of help.

Your Eldorado Travel were most obliging but couldn't provide much information so long after the event. They have no details of the transaction other than an entry in their books which doesn't help very much. However they are what I believe is nowadays called a 'bucket shop', specialising in cheap flights to Spain and Latin America. From the sum involved they feel sure it must have been for one of their flights to Spain but it could have been to one of several destinations. They work with a number of charter carriers, and couldn't be sure now which one was involved. All in all, not a great deal of help to you, I imagine.

Yes, such a shame about the meal but I shall certainly try to get up to London again in the not too distant future. At the moment I am heavily involved in my capacity as legal adviser to the local branch of the NFU - all this BSE nonsense. What a wretched mess!

Yours affectionately,

G

Spain!

A letter was hastily penned to Enid, asking if she could kindly send us Rupert's card. Whilst waiting for the reply, I would meanwhile undertake some research at Hamers in the hope of tying up a few loose ends.

The results of our market surveys went for analysis to the Statistics Department, known as Stats, which was run virtually single-handed and with great efficiency by Robert. Robert was an awkward, gangly youth who could barely string two words together but with computers he was a wizard.

He was also more than willing to run through his database with me and leave me to browse through his records.

After a few false starts I was quickly able to produce a schedule of all the surveys on which Rupert had worked, together with dates and locations of the interviews he had conducted. The number of returns and the analyses were of no interest to me. What was of interest but no longer came as a surprise was the fact that Rupert had been working in London immediately before the weekend of the accident and had filed his returns on the Friday afternoon before leaving to meet us in Overton.

Robert confirmed that Hamers' surveys were invariably conducted by contract interviewers. Any interviews in Manchester, or anywhere else for that matter, would have been handled by local people. Imagine the cost of having to put up your interviewers in hotels and pay their expenses.

So Manchester, it seemed, had been part of his fantasy world as had been the name Rupert Cunningham and the title of Senior Account Manager, or was this putting too innocent a gloss on it?

The card arrived from Aunt Enid some weeks later, and was even more bent than before. It had become mislaid, she explained, and took a while to find. Regrettably, it told us no more than it had the first time. We pored over the postmark but were at a loss to decipher it. So with no great optimism, Beck undertook to show it to a Spanish lady in the Iberian Section at work, and came back some days later with the information that the traditional costume worn by the small girl was typical of those found in Catalonia, and still worn today on holidays and feast days. That didn't mean to say that you couldn't buy a card like this anywhere in Spain, with the possible exception of the northern Basque territory.

"Well done, Watson," I said, with heavy sarcasm, puffing smugly on the handle of a teaspoon representing my favourite briar. "Let's look at the facts of the case as we know them," said whilst stabbing the air with the teaspoon handle for added emphasis. "Our chap shuts up shop after the funeral and hops it to Spain. So far, so good. I accept that the evidence for this is circumstantial - the counterfoil for the air ticket and the post card - but it's a reasonable enough assumption. Where exactly did he go to in Spain? The card suggests it might have been Eastern Spain. But you can't rule out Southern Spain, or even Central Spain, either. And don't forget, dear Watson, this all happened well over a year ago. Add to this the fact that we don't even know what name he's using. Why, the scoundrel could be anywhere by now, getting up to God knows what mischief."

Watson was unimpressed with my analysis. God, did we need a break.

It was Sara who taught me Naughty Cuddles. That was in Exeter, after Worcester. It's funny how you think of these things when you haven't much else on your mind.

She shared a house with three other girls and their various boy friends. It was a bit run-down, an Edwardian semi - it would have been quite smart in its day. There was always lots going on, comings and goings and parties and stuff. And there was always food and drink even if you did have to scrape the mould off the bread and wash up a cup and plate before you could use them.

My main job was at the petrol station as cashier. I did some bar work as well. I didn't earn much but I gave Sara what I could towards the housekeeping. I don't suppose she really needed it but it made me feel better anyway.

What also made me feel better, a lot better, was Naughty Cuddles. That was a new game Sara taught me.

She allowed me to share her bed at the house. It was a double and I was happy just to snuggle up to her at night. Her smell reminded me of Mummy and all I wanted was to curl up inside her tummy and be protected from all the bad things in the world. At first I didn't want to play her game but after it was over, I really liked it, I really did. In fact I wanted to play it all the time. Tim and I had played mummies and daddies as boys - Tim was older than me so he was always the daddy - but we were only going through the motions, as it were. We didn't realise that we hadn't got the right bits.

With Sara it was quite different and I would try to bribe her with Smarties but she would tease me, hiding them about her person, as they say, and making me find and eat them without using my hands. After that we'd have Naughty Cuddles.

Why me? Why me? Why me? Why me?

That is the question which, like everyone else in this situation, I asked myself repeatedly in those days and weeks.

My problem became common knowledge after the blackout at work and could no longer be ignored. The second one at home, soon after, was the clincher. I was bristling with aggression as I walked into Dr. Singh's surgery. This time, I was not going to be fobbed off and sent home with a few pills. However, I didn't need to resort to any histrionics; the good doctor saw straight away that this was no mere question of blood pressure and, after a thorough examination, arranged for a blood test and brain scan.

By the time the appointed day came, I was a total nervous wreck. Beck was most supportive and came with me in the mini-cab to the hospital. I don't know whether it's normal practice to lash the patient to the trolley before being inserted into the scanner, or whether it was only necessary in my case to stop the shaking and avoid blurring the image. I have always had an aversion to anything medical and must be the world's worst patient. The ordeal over, I then had to wait a further few nerve-wracking days for my appointment with the consultant to learn the results.

My brain just wasn't in gear as he showed me the images and patiently explained the results. His words became censored, leaving only those spelling doom and gloom, like growth, pressure, mood swings, anxiety, malignant, serious concern, prognosis. Consequently, I completely misinterpreted his remarks and would have remained under this misapprehension had Beck not been there too and able to explain it all later.

Yes, the scan had shown a shadow, which was likely to be some form of growth. This would exert pressure on part of the brain and account for the blackouts. They needed to take a closer look under general anaesthetic and obtain a sample for analysis. This would involve being admitted for one or two days and would help establish whether the growth was malignant or benign. The appropriate course of treatment could then be decided. The good news was that it was in an operable position and had, apparently, been caught at an early stage. Either way, the prognosis so far was good and didn't give cause for serious concern.

I was floating on my back on a glass-like sea, looking up into the sun. It required no effort to stay afloat and the water was warm. Turning my head, I could see Beck floating like me, her magnificent hair fanned out on the surface of the water, like an aurora. On the other side lay Sara, reciting what sounded like a love poem, her bronzed body glistening in the sun. Rupert was naked but for his scarf, with a little boy's willy bobbing on the surface like a cork. The sight of it made me start to laugh. Suddenly, into the middle of our circle burst George Bulstrode, rising vertically out of the water where he continued to float upright like a buoy, his hair perfectly dry and in place. The waves caused by his unexpected appearance washed over my face causing me to choke. I felt myself sinking and began to struggle but couldn't move. Then I thought I saw Beck smiling at me, and my mother.

I finally regained consciousness to find the room empty. My limbs felt like lead, and there were wires and tubes everywhere. This is what it must feel like to be a marionette, I thought, unable to move without someone to pull your strings. But it wasn't long before a passing nurse noticed I was awake and brought a cup of tea, staying to help me drink it. Whatever the jokes about hospital tea, this was surely the best cuppa I have ever tasted.

Later still, the consultant came to see me. The news was good, very good. The tumour was deemed to be benign and whilst I was anaesthetised, he had decided to go ahead and remove it straight away. With any luck I should be out and back on my feet again within a few days. This time there was no auto-censor at work - I took in what was said first time. When Beck came with Mum I couldn't get out the news for crying.

"I've seen him."

"Seen who?" she wanted to know. Beck was on one of her many hospital visits in those days after the operation.

"Rupert, of course. I had a vision."

Perhaps vision was too strong a word but I had seen him, several times in fact, whilst drifting in and out of consciousness.

“You had a vision. You, who blew our chance of reaching Sara through the seance, you had a vision.”

“Yes, I did. I saw him.”

“OK. So how was he, and did he have much to say, any message or anything?”

“Look, I’m sorry about the seance and I did apologise to Irena at the time. But things are different now. And no, he didn’t have any message.”

I could understand Beck’s cynicism but Rupert really had appeared to me, or perhaps it would be more accurate to say I dreamt of him. The first time, there had been the water, then there was the stately home set in parkland. I had glimpsed it from a distance through the trees but the rider emerging from the courtyard at the rear wasn’t at first recognisable. Yet as it approached there was no mistaking the figure of Rupert and his characteristic dress. He didn’t see me and passed from view before I could attract his attention. Every detail of the house was fixed in my memory though, and I was sure I could identify it from a picture and even draw it, if asked.

The third and last sighting was even more vivid. Rupert was no longer in his usual attire. Gone were the mustard-coloured trousers and there was no trace of the scarf either. Instead he was dressed in a grey shirt and baggy, elasticated trousers. He was in a small room, the furnishings minimal, and although there was a view from the window on to some kind of garden, the glass was re-enforced with wire and the frame sealed.

Rupert himself sat crouched on the edge of the

bed, leaning forward, elbows on knees. Unshaven, he looked pale and drawn. I called out his name but my voice was too weak to penetrate the thick glass in the small inspection window. When he did eventually look up, his eyes were bloodshot and glazed. I called again, but even looking directly at me, his face showed no signs of recognition. Eventually I turned away.

Beck had listened to this account with an expression ranging from scepticism to shock.

"Well......." was all she could manage, temporarily lost for words. "Where do we go from here?"

As it happened, we didn't need to go anywhere - yet.

Espana

Greetings peasants!

Still enjoying life here. Sun, Sea, and Sangrilla and even a bit of the other if I'm lucky!

Hasta la Vista!

Rupert

The card had arrived whilst I was still in hospital and, although the message itself was innocuous enough, even inane, it at last provided a positive lead in the search for Rupert.

Like the first card, this one too bore no date, but

this time the postmark was clearly legible. Beck had already done her homework. The card had been posted nearly two weeks ago in Balduras, a small town with a population of 3280, situated in the South Eastern corner of Spain, just inland from the coast and not far from the border with France. Pictured on the card was the Playa de las Americas, further down the Costa Brava towards Barcelona.

What was less easily established was Rupert's motive in writing to us. He obviously intended us to know he still existed, but why didn't he provide an address if we were expected to contact him? Was he taunting us? Was this another childish game - of hide and seek? Be that as it may, two years of dashing about had established nothing, other than the fact that Rupert was dishonest and was not to be found. But now we had something to go on.

Things are different now, I had said to Beck, and meant it. The prospect of having your life cut short changes your values and adds a sense of urgency to everything. Whilst ill, people had shown immense kindness towards me. My mother had been emotional, as you would expect, but Uncle Clive had kept an eye on her, and Mark had come all the way from York with Anne and the kids. Beck too had been brilliant and people at work, and at the rowing club, had sent cards and flowers. Even dear Aunt Enid, who must have heard the news from Beck, had written to wish me a speedy recovery. She had wanted to send fruit or flowers, bless her, but didn't know how to go about it and whether she could afford it - she only had her pension to live on.

As I lay there during those long days after the operation, my life crowded in on me and I vowed, if I escaped the jaws of death, to repay the kindness bestowed on me and atone for my sins of omission and past misdeeds. Not least of my intentions was to devote myself body and soul to the search for Rupert. But as so often, the hand of fortune intervened first - this time in the guise of Quentin. Quentin was a veritable Adonis, a dream, a vision, and unavailable. As his wife, I wouldn't be able to sleep at night, knowing that every female with an atom of hormone left in her body would be lusting after his. But I'm getting carried away.

Quentin Roper was Beck's man in Spain, and based in Madrid. I had been introduced to him at a rather pretentious party in London. It was not long after being discharged from hospital and, in my clumsy, provincial way, I probably made something of a fool of myself. However it came about, I found myself alone in conversation with this cultivated man and talking more than I should, to hide my nerves. As I gushed, a spot of spittle, to my horror, landed on his lapel. My instinct was to reach out and sponge it off, but Quentin, perceiving my embarrassment, displayed the impeccable manners of his class. As my speech faltered, he quickly interjected an observation of his own, to maintain the flow of conversation, allowing me time to recover my composure and the spot to soak in, leaving a barely perceptible stain.

With the last card from Spain still occupying my

thoughts, I explained how, and why, we urgently needed to contact Rupert, and ventured to ask Quentin if, with his Iberian connections, he could possibly help track him down. He actually knew the Balduras area quite well, in fact a friend of his had a holiday apartment there. He volunteered to arrange for us to stay there for a few days, so we could make on-the-spot enquiries. This, he felt sure, would be the best plan of attack. If his commitments allowed, he would try to join us, provided, that is, we felt he could be of any assistance. Fortunately, Beck appeared just in time to hear and graciously accept this amazing offer, which left me a stammering wreck.

The hunt was on.

Dear diary,
Day 1.

Flat OK. Feeling jaded after journey. Spent day getting bearings. Found supermercado and did shopping. Ate in and crashed out at 9 o'clock. Getting old!

We landed at Gerona airport at the ungodly hour of 3.30 in the morning. My hair had grown back to a reasonable length in the eight weeks since leaving hospital, and the consultant had pronounced me fit to travel. At Hamers, my boss had been marvellous and left it to me to come back to work, as and when I felt well enough. So there we were, for seven whole days, two single girls with but one mission.

I feared the worst, on learning that we were going to the Costa Brava - visions of head-to-toe beaches, with barely an inch of sand to be seen between the miles of sweating, lobster-coloured flesh. And sure enough, the pints of lager and back-to-front baseball caps were already in evidence, as we waited for the flight at Gatwick. But on arrival, the hordes headed off in their coaches in one direction and we, in our little hired Fiat, thankfully in the other.

Unfortunately, the key to the apartment had to be picked up from a local estate agent whose office didn't open until 10 o'clock. So, like two drop-outs or, as Beck put it, two beached whales, we stretched out on the vast, empty beach and dozed as the first rays of the sun reached over the horizon, bringing their welcome warmth.

My misgivings about the area also proved misplaced. There were no high-rise hotels, no teeming masses. The only evidence of a tourist industry was on a modest scale in the form of a campsite and a rather tasteful holiday village. What housing there was comprised of large villas, discreetly set in their own grounds amongst the pines, and bearing names such as Bella Vista and Casa Muller.

Our apartment occupied the ground floor of a modern, semi-detached house, standing on the hill behind the local fishing village, and approximately three miles from Balduras, the village where Rupert's card had been posted. The interior was cool and spartan, but more than adequate for our needs - we weren't planning on spending much time indoors.

Day 2

Made sortie into Balduras to enquire about Rupert. No joy. Spent afternoon on beach and had dinner in village. Bought dictionary.

Situated on a hilltop, Balduras was an attractive village, dominated by a ruined fortification. The houses huddled beneath were, for the most part, painted in cream and pastel shades, with violent splashes of colour made by the window boxes, cascading with geraniums. In holiday mood, we decided first to have coffee in the little square, and absorb the atmosphere. The pace was slow and, at this time of the day, the population seemed to be made up almost entirely of stooped, little old ladies dressed in black. The occasional pick-up came to fetch or deliver, causing the tabby, asleep in the road, to grudgingly yield its territory. Two young mothers disappeared into the tiny supermarket, leaving their off-spring to enjoy the morning sun in their pushchairs outside. The male population must be out at work, we concluded, and the children at school.

It was reasonable to assume that, in this environment, the passing tourist would not arouse undue interest. But any outsider who began to appear regularly, using the post office or bank, for example, would surely be remembered, especially out of season. This being the case, we embarked on our task in a mood of some optimism.

On Beck's CV she laid claim to a working knowledge of Spanish. After her painful interrogation of the locals that morning, I questioned just what sort of work she had in mind. Speaking from a position of superior ignorance, I both mocked and squirmed with embarrassment, in turn. The only person with whom we were able to make ourselves halfway understood was the counter clerk at the bank, and only then because he spoke some English. But his patience was quickly exhausted when he learned that we had lost our friend - stupid English! All in all, a fruitless exercise.

The search abandoned for the rest of the day, we switched to tourist mode, which meant that, when not eating and drinking, we lay on the beach in the sun.

Day 3

Sightseeing along coast. Visited ruins of vast Roman city. Most impressive. Too much Rioja at lunchtime - some people never learn!

Our quest for Rupert temporarily suspended, hopes were pinned on Quentin, due to arrive next day from Madrid. Meanwhile, we took the opportunity to explore the coast in our little car, visiting the fishing villages and ending up with a wonderful seafood lunch in a tiny restaurant, packed with locals. On an empty stomach, the wine went straight to my head, leaving me with a headache for the rest of the day, despite an improvised siesta.

The ruined city of Apulia we more or less stumbled on by chance, which made the visit all the more memorable. Without the benefit of a guide, half the enjoyment came in trying to guess the function of some of the smaller, excavated chambers. Eventually, the combined effects of lunch and fatigue took their toll and we dragged ourselves back to our temporary home.

Day 4

Waiting for Quentin!!

I spent the day in quivering anticipation of the arrival of Quentin that evening. After a late start, we camped out on the beach for the morning, before embarking on a walk after a picnic lunch.

From the beach, the cliff path climbed steeply through the pines before reaching the headland and turning in towards the next bay. Looking down over the edge, the surprise of what I saw caused me to stub my toe painfully against a rock. There, a hundred or more feet beneath us, lying on the clean-washed sand, was a couple, completely naked. Fascinated, Beck had to drag me away, observing from an apparent position of superior knowledge how Latin types always seemed to be so much better endowed than their North European counterparts. I guessed she was referring to the male of the species.

As the path dropped to a lower level and turned a

corner, all became revealed, literally. The next bay was reserved for nude bathing and we, whether we liked it or not, were provided with a balcony view. All sorts and conditions of men, women and children were busying themselves with normal beach activities, unself-conscious in their natural-born state. But we couldn't conceal our surprise, on being approached from the opposite direction by a middle-aged male figure, dressed only in flip-flops and a skimpy T-shirt. "Guten Tag," it said in passing, locking our eyes with a knowing stare. We struck off at the first opportunity to rejoin the road and hasten back to the car.

Later that evening, having overcome our culture shock with the help of a bottle of wine, we fantasised about the possibility of inviting Quentin to join us on our new-found beach.

The meal we had lovingly prepared was ruined by the time dream-man finally arrived in a petulant mood, having driven round in the dark for an hour, trying to find the flat. This wasn't the romantic re-union I had visualised. But, fixed up with a large scotch, he calmed down sufficiently to accept our offer of an omelette - Spanish, of course, ha, ha!

The next day found Quentin in a much better frame of mind, despite what must have been an uncomfortable night on the sofa. Over breakfast, we discussed our strategy for the day ahead, the plan being to go back to Balduras, this time however armed with our fluent Spanish speaker.

All the places where Rupert might have called were duly revisited in the course of the morning.

Later, over a sandwich and a beer at the beach café, we reviewed what had been a most satisfactory morning's work. This time, our efforts had brought an almost immediate reward.

The *señora* at the mini-supermarket definitely remembered a blond-haired young Englishman. Arriving with his friends as he had, in winter, his dress hadn't attracted attention at first but, as winter eventually turned into spring and spring into summer, The English Boy still wore his scarf. Crazy English!

Rupert. This had to be Rupert.

Sometimes he would be alone, sometimes accompanied by one or more of his friends. They still shopped there occasionally, but she hadn't seen the crazy one for some time. Payment was always in cash and the *señora* had never been asked to deliver, so didn't know where they lived - probably in one of the villas. Asked what sort of car they drove, she thought it was Spanish-registered - possibly a Fiat but wasn't very well up on cars. The colour was electric blue, that she did remember. No worthwhile description of the friends was forthcoming - the English all looked the same, and you get so many in the summer.

"Another beer? " offered Quentin.

"Why not!"

The beers ordered and the first draught downed with a sigh of satisfaction: "Any idea who these friends might be?" Quentin's question was met with a stony silence.

"Um. Well, we might not have achieved much but at least I hope I've been of some small help to you, that you manage to find him. I don't know what your own immediate plans are, Beck and Phil, but I think I ought to be getting back to Madrid tonight - got quite a lot on at the moment........."

"Rupert could still be around, of course," I interrupted, not wanting to hear what Quentin was saying, "Just doing his shopping and things somewhere else."

Nobody picked up on my contribution.

"What I find surprising is that they don't know him at the bank. I mean, what does he do for money? Supposing he has cash, English money, that is, he still has to change it somewhere, doesn't he? At the supermarket she said he always paid cash - that means pesetas," offered Beck.

No-one had an answer to this either.

"I think we should leave a note for him at the *supermercado,*" Quentin proposed, "in case he does show up there again. What do you think?"

Not a brilliant suggestion, but coming as it did from our idol, the proposal was adopted and a note duly scribbled and given to the *señora,* when the shop re-opened later. Addressed to Rupert, we offered a few platitudinous snippets of news and asked him to contact us, giving our London address. Time would tell.

Quentin was persuaded to stay and travel back to Madrid the following day. The bait was a thank-you meal at the best restaurant in the area and the company of two charming young ladies (Beck and me). But I think it was more the lateness of the hour which decided it. Be that as it may, we basked in the presence of our handsome, witty and charming chaperone, who next day was gone before our tousled heads were off the pillow.

"You lookin' for Rupert?" the voice asked.

We were sitting at the beach café for what had become a regular lunchtime beer and roll, having spent the morning fruitlessly camped out in the café, opposite the supermarket.

"Only 'e's not 'ere," the voice continued quickly.

Turning round in surprise, a large slice of tomato fell out of my roll and landed with a slap on the plate. Under any other circumstances, this would have detracted from the drama of the moment. Right now, it went unnoticed.

For an instant, both Beck and I were at a loss for words. The questioner was a young man, possibly no more than 17 or 18, wearing stylish long shorts, loafers and a pale green vest which left his angular shoulder blades exposed at the back. He was slightly built, almost wiry, tanned, with close-cropped hair and sporting an earring. The accent placed him somewhere in Essex.

"Yes, we are friends of Rupert, but......... "

"Right. Well I'm Kev and Rupert's not 'ere. He's gone, you see."

"Well, er, Kev, why don't you join us for a beer and then you can tell us all about Rupert."

(This, Watson, is a New Development in the case

and must be handled with consummate skill. Leave this to me.)

"So, Kevin, you know Rupert then?" I asked. (This is what is known in the textbooks as a leading question, designed to draw out the interviewee.)

"No. I never!"

Beck took over: "But you do know who we are talking about?"

"Oh yeah. Good bloke, Rupert."

"OK. So we've established that we are all talking about the same person, singing from the same hymn sheet, so to speak, yes?" Beck breaking into one of her winning smiles.

Kev nodded and took a large swig of his beer. I didn't think he and Beck were talking the same language at all. To me, Kev was a half-wit.

"So, if Rupert's not here," Beck paused to allow Kev to grasp and tacitly confirm this point, "where is he?" Beck leant forward, still smiling but pressing for a reply.

"I dunno. I was just told to say he ain't 'ere."

Kev's defence wasn't difficult to break down. Beck quickly latched onto this slip, moving in for the kill.

"Who told you to say that, Kevin? Come on, who?"

"Tim. It was Tim. Oh God, 'e'll kill me." Kev started to sob, rubbing his reddened eyes. His dirty fingernails were chewed short, I noticed, and his hands were small and stubby, like a child's.

Beck's front never showed a crack at the enormity of this disclosure. Having broken Kev, she now cleverly switched her tone to one of compassion, in order to drive home her advantage. This was a masterful performance, the pupil instructing the teacher.

"Come on, Kev. It can't be all that bad. Here, take my hanky." I made a mental note to remind Beck to burn it afterwards. "I'll square it with Tim, tell him it wasn't your fault. We're old friends of Tim too, you know."

Capitalising on Kev's emotional state, we quickly called for the bill and, hardly allowing him time to finish his beer, dragged the hapless youth away to lead us to Tim.

It was only later, that we had time to pause for breath and analyse the situation. Meanwhile, we were being swept along by events at an unprecedented pace. We may be no nearer finding Rupert but *Tim*..........This could only be Sara's Tim.

To ensure that Kev didn't suffer a change of heart, Beck cleverly elected to ride pillion on his scooter, creating a kind of reverse hostage situation. I followed in the Fiat. Our journey probably didn't take us more than three miles but it seemed much longer and I had to grip the wheel to stop my hands from shaking. In effect, we were re-tracing our route of two days previously, following the winding road, just inland from the coast. On the hills, Kevin's scooter slowed almost to a halt, leaving behind it a slowly dispersing trail of blue smoke. After what seemed an age, we finally turned into a side road, followed by a sandy track, before arriving at the gates of a white-painted villa, set among the pines.

It was hard to say, at first sight, how large the property was. A single storey building, it appeared to cover a considerable area and was relatively new. After dismounting, Kev chose not to enter the house from the front but set off round the side. Did Beck's knees buckle slightly as she got off the scooter, or was it cramp? I was certainly nervous as hell, and my mouth felt dry, as we tagged along after Kev.

The sight that greeted us as we rounded the corner brought us up with a jolt. Lying in the sun, on a lounger by the pool, was an all-male figure whose only item of apparel was a pair of sunglasses.

"Shit!" it muttered, leaping up and running barefoot for cover, pale buttocks flapping pathetically in the sun. Kev followed indoors like a dog, knowing it was about to be beaten. Whilst Beck and I stood around awkwardly, punishment was duly being dished out on the unfortunate Kevin. From the few whispered words we were able to exchange, it was clear that neither of us felt absolutely sure that the disturbed sunbather had in fact been Sara's Tim.

The man who emerged a little later had not only recovered his composure but also re-covered his parts. A firm, dry hand was extended to welcome us, backed by a warm smile.

"Hi girls," he said. "I'm sorry. I wasn't expecting visitors. Ha ha!" The forced laugh, intended to cover any remaining traces of embarrassment, betrayed tension. "I think we've met before. I'm Tim."

Ushered to a table on the terrace, where a puffy-eyed Kev brought drinks, we had time to weigh up 'Tim'.

My recollection of Sara's brother was of a besuited character wearing a pink-striped shirt and red and white polka-dot tie, the slightly greasy hair parted at the side, brushed straight, and crowning an equally greasy, if not pimply, complexion. The voice was the same, but New Tim otherwise bore little resemblance to the old. This was literally a leaner, but fitter-looking Tim. Any flab, from over-indulgence in the commodities in which he might previously have traded, had completely disappeared. The hair, cut short and brushed forward to hide a receding hairline, was bleached by the sun to a straw colour, whilst the now slight body was tanned to an enviable, uniform honey colour.

Beck took charge of the preliminary small-talk. She discreetly introduced our names into the conversation, in case Tim had forgotten them - this was only the third time we had met him. At the same time, we mutually agreed that our last meeting had been on the sad occasion of the funeral.

Beck initially chose to steer clear of the subject of Rupert.

"So what decided you to come to Spain, Tim? I mean, is this it? Do you plan to stay here permanently? It's a glorious spot, isn't it? Can't say I blame you," even Beck's nerves were beginning to show; she was starting to gabble.

"Sorry," she finished feebly, apologising for nothing in particular.

Tim didn't prevaricate and needed no prompting. Over the course of the next two hours, he quietly and calmly told us everything we needed to know.

Just occasionally, a trace of emotion would show, especially when talking of Sara and their childhood together.

Although Tim and Sara had rather drifted apart since leaving home, they had been very close as children and such bonds remain throughout your life, even if time and circumstances should lead you down separate paths. Equally, Tim was conscious of having neglected Gloria in later years, partly because he disapproved of her private life. But the ties between mother and child are unbreakable and, when both Gloria and Sara died on the same day, in such harrowing circumstances, the bottom fell out of Tim's world. Once the funeral was over, and the distressing formalities dealt with, he felt the overwhelming urge to get away. You have to understand that the pressure was immense, and he desperately needed space and time to re-build his life.

A momentary pause in the narrative enabled me to glance across at Beck. Like me, she was clearly affected by this account.

It might seem a complete overreaction, and possibly it was, but Tim decided to quit both job and flat, and just take off. With no clear plan, he vaguely thought to travel to the Far East, possibly ending up in Australia, or even New Zealand. He had met people through work who had travelled in India, Thailand and China, and come back with glowing accounts. You only get one life, so what the hell.

Exactly what led Tim to Spain and this particular spot he couldn't explain. We may have heard that he had been the main beneficiary under Gloria's will and, although it pained him to even think, and still more, to talk about it, it's one of those facts of life that have to be faced. Tim would give anything to show Gloria how he had spent the money - he knew she would approve. He could understand those people who genuinely believe they can communicate with the dead, and would dearly join them if he thought for a moment it would work. It's such a shame you can't retrieve people from the beyond, even if only for short periods - like borrowing a book from the library or taking a relative away from the retirement home, for a holiday. He would love to have Gloria to stay.

This spoken with a sad, wry half-smile. I could feel a lump rising in my throat - I felt just the same way about my father, and wanted to say so. I stopped myself just in time, for fear of looking foolish in front of Beck. I am sure Tim would have understood.

At the funeral, Tim had recognised in Rupert a kindred spirit. Rupert's bonds with the deceased had been almost as strong as his own and the emotions they experienced were identical. After Tim was settled in Spain, he invited Rupert to come out and join him for a holiday. When he arrived, Tim was shocked to find that he too had sacrificed a good job, while clearly undergoing a severe emotional trauma. His financial resources were practically non-existent but, for the sake of his former friendship with Sara, Tim was willing to give him a roof over his head until he found his feet again.

"I don't know how much you know about Rupert," Tim said, "but he's not a very strong character. Please don't misunderstand me, I'm very fond of Rupert, he's a dear friend. But I have to say that, in my view, it was Sara who propped him up. In fact, without our family I think, one way or another, he would have gone to pieces. If you want an example, just look at the time he spent on his own, after Sara went away to college. That was a near disaster."

"What happened?" we both asked at the same time. Tim had us hanging on his every word by now.

"Well, I can't tell you all the details. All I know is that he couldn't hold down a steady job and got into some pretty bad company."

"So where is he now?" Finally, the question we had been dying to ask.

Before answering, Tim shouted at stupid Kevin to bring out more drinks.

"He went to the Fatherland after a bit of skirt, if you can believe it. I couldn't stop him; he was determined to go. Poor Rupert discovered the nudist beach, you see - I don't know if you've been there. Absolutely fascinated by it, down there every day. Anyway, he brought these two German birds back one day, like a dog that'd found two bones - one for him and one for me. Well, he got that bit wrong - I've never liked German women. They're far too dominating for me. I prefer a woman to be more feminine, submissive, if you know what I mean."

"How long ago was this, Tim?" We didn't want him elaborating on his favourite type of submission.

"Oh, some time last summer, I suppose."

"And have you heard from him since? Have you got an address?"

"I may have. He did send a card, but quite honestly I've washed my hands of the foolish boy. He's got to make his own way now."

Eventually an address was produced which we duly wrote down and the official interview, or audience, over and the sun rapidly setting, the informal proceedings now began. Tim skilfully lit a barbecue and equally skilfully entertained us for the rest of the evening, Kevin waiting on. He proved to be an accomplished host and good company too, once the tension had evaporated, and we left quite late to pack our things, ready for the drive to the airport next day.

Days 5,6,7.

No time to write. Met Tim of all people! He had out-dated news of R. but our quarry still remains elusive.

Back to the smoke.

"Rubbish!" said Beck. "Absolute tosh! You were taken in by him, Phil, we both were. He played with us - toyed with our emotions."

We were sitting over dinner at the flat, after our first day back at work.

"He's hiding something," Beck continued. "I don't believe a word about that German girl and I bet that address doesn't even exist either. Did you notice how he pretended he couldn't find it at first? I thought that was very clever. If you ask me, Rupert is still around, in hiding for whatever reason. Why else should he send that dim-witted lad to find us and put us off the scent? After all, we had the post card from him, from Balduras, just a couple of weeks ago."

Beck was getting quite irate now.

"And all that business about asking Rupert to join him - after the funeral. It just doesn't stack up."

She went on to point out that we had conclusive proof that Rupert had made a flight booking to Spain *before* the accident. The actual date of the flight was immaterial - it was *pre-planned*, that was the point.

My contention was that this was purely circumstantial - I leaned more to Tim's account. It had only been *suggested* that the credit card coupon was for a flight to Spain. It might have been for something else entirely. Or it could have been a deposit on *two* tickets - for himself and Sara, for a summer holiday. There was no way of knowing.

My cool, calm voice of reason: Rupert might have returned to the Balduras area, unknown to Tim - after all, the supermarket owner hadn't seen him for some time - or just paid a brief visit, to collect some things, say. Or he may be deliberately lying low, for whatever reason. From his standpoint, Tim could be telling the truth. But Beck was adamant. There was something fishy going on and she was going to get to the bottom of it.

Despite these polarised views, our emotional attitude towards Rupert himself swung from affection for a friend, at one extreme, to anger at his irresponsible and selfish behaviour, at the other. This made the task of writing even more difficult. Disregarding Beck's scepticism, I took it upon myself to write to Rupert care of his bit of Teutonic skirt, as Tim had so indelicately put it. But even I didn't rate the chances of a reply very highly, yet it seemed the only available course of action following the visit to Spain.

Dear Rupert,

Many thanks for your card from Spain. In fact we met Tim there recently which is how we came by your new address. He told us a little about what you have been up to but we would dearly like to hear all your news first hand.

Do you realise that we haven't seen you since the day of the funeral? We were all absolutely devastated by what happened and could have used your support at the time and could in turn have offered you ours. But it's no good going over old ground and we have to look to the future now, which is exactly what you seem to have done in going to Germany and making a new start. How do you like life over there and what are you doing for a living?

Do write soon! Beck sends her love too.

Phil XXX

The wound on my thigh is more like a bloody chasm than just a gash. It actually gapes at you, you can see right down inside. At first you wonder why there's no blood, not even raw flesh on the sides. But look again and you see that the creamy matter is moving, kind of pulsating. It's a heaving, bloody living organism with hundreds of tiny, headless bodies - like squirming fat grubs, feeding off your own rotting flesh, my fucking flesh!

But the funny thing is, there's no pain, just a gentle sensation that's hard to describe. If I push the maggots to one side with my finger I can see the dry white bone and tendons. And they squash easily too. They leave a milky yellow stain and a strange smell on your fingers.

Because you've got no clothes on, just lying on this kind of rubber sheet, you can't help sweating. The wood lice like it nice and warm and damp. Whole bloody families of them - Mummy, Daddy and a tribe of bloody kids. Some of the cheeky bastards come out to eat the pus that's oozing from those black sores on my legs. The rest are just happy to feed on the bacteria between my toes. That's where those matt black jobs live too. They look like miniature scorpion. You can't squash them, not even between the nails of your thumb and first finger. The only way to kill them is to bite them in two but the taste makes you want to throw up. Even then the two halves run around on their own for a bit.

But none of this upsets me, not really. What really does get to me, though, is the ants. They do my head in. I just crack up, go to pieces. I can't bloody move, just lie there paralysed. Like bloody armies, three of them, three bloody armies, marching in single file up my legs. The pain is killing. When they reach my balls, I usually heave up, everywhere. That distracts them for a bit but then more and more come - until you can't see me at all, just a mass of teaming fucking ants. In the end my head hurts so much it just explodes and everything goes black.

7

The baby might have been six or eight weeks old. It couldn't have been there more than a couple of hours. Bundled up in a carry-cot, it was waiting for me on the doorstep when I returned from work. On seeing me, its little face screwed up and turned red, as if to cry, but relaxed again after a moment, without a sound. Up and down the street, life was going on as normal; nobody appeared to be watching, or waiting, and all the parked cars were empty. More than a little unnerved, I stepped round the carry-cot and let myself in. Some twenty minutes later, my mind racing, I was on the point of calling the police when I heard, simultaneously, the sound of Beck letting herself in and the baby crying.

"Taken up baby snatching, have we?" asked Beck facetiously. "Who on earth does *that* belong to?"

I told her what little there was to tell. "Better get on with it then. Call them!" was Beck's response.

But the ever more persistent crying of the baby demanded a more immediate and humanitarian response. Already an aunt herself, Beck's maternal instincts finally took over and, bringing in the carry-cot, she expertly gathered up the poor mite and comforted it with little cooing noises. It was then that we saw the envelope.

Hallo you!

He is belonging to the Rupert. This also is his name. When you are seeing him, please to overhand him the baby with many loves from
Your Sabine Schmitz

My God! This was Rupert's child - Baby Rupert.

His parentage revealed, Baby started to cry again, but this time more loudly. Ever the practical one, Beck despatched me to the corner shop for baby food and a supply of disposable nappies. After his meal, a nappy change and a few burps, our little charge gave us a winning smile, which instantly endeared him to both of us. Cradling him contentedly on one arm and skilfully pouring a glass of wine with the other, Beck convened a council of elders to discuss the future of Baby.

Like me, her initial response had been to inform the police. But the wider implications now had to be considered. Clearly, the address produced by Tim hadn't been a blind and Sabine, presumably the mother and Rupert's German girlfriend, must have intercepted my letter, so obtaining our address. Beyond this, we knew nothing about her, her circumstances nor why she had abandoned the baby. She might conceivably be suffering from post-natal depression and in need of help. If we handed him over to the authorities, details would have to be provided of the mother, otherwise the child could become lost in the system and Sabine never have the chance to see him again. On the other hand, to disclose her name and address, without her permission, could get her into all sorts of trouble. Supposing she were a teenager, living with her parents and still at school, or even married with a husband.

And what of Rupert Senior? He had seemingly left his German girlfriend, literally, holding the baby and could end up with a paternity suit against him. But then, why shouldn't he face up to his responsibilities? One thing was clear. There was no way in which we could look after young Rupert, not even for a few days. God, what a mess!

It was approaching midnight, when we both simultaneously hit on the idea of taking our problem to Enid, in the truest sense. If she could only look after Baby for a few days, whilst we sorted things out.......

Next day, with no time for formalities, we phoned our respective offices, picked up a hire car, and set off with Baby for Herefordshire. The whole venture was a gamble, firstly finding Enid at home and, more importantly, receptive.

Surprised at seeing us on her doorstep unannounced, Enid quickly gathered herself and invited us in. She was even more surprised when Beck, on the pretext of fetching something from the car, appeared some moments later clutching Baby. Mrs. C. automatically assumed the baby to be Beck's and became dewy-eyed, as the supposed mother cleverly got her to hold him. He, for his part, performed superbly, responding warmly to Enid's motherly charms.

In this cosy situation, we set about explaining who Baby was, and exactly why we had come. This meant telling Enid everything about our quest for Rupert but, long before we got to the ultimate reason for the visit, it was clear that the poor lady was thoroughly confused.

"So, who's this German woman, then? What's she got to do with it?" Enid wanted to know.

"Sabine is the baby's mother," Beck patiently explained.

"But you said it was your baby. You are lucky – he's just gorgeous, isn't he?"

"Yes, he is, Enid, but he's not mine. You must have misunderstood. I haven't got a baby. Sabine really is the mother."

"Well, what's that got to do with my Brian and why have you got him?"

At first Enid didn't want to accept that Rupert was the father and steadfastly refused to countenance the fact. That the barrier had finally been breached was evidenced by the silent tears, which began to run down her cheeks as she tightly hugged the baby.

"The poor lamb," she whispered, gently rocking backwards and forwards. "The poor little lamb."

At that moment, we knew we had won.

With the immediate problem temporarily solved, speed was now of the essence. Village busy-bodies might start asking questions and Enid couldn't be expected to look after Baby indefinitely. The irony of the situation could not have escaped her - Baby Rupert, himself the product of an unwanted baby, and both dumped on good old Aunt Enid.

From whatever motive, Rupert had obviously walked out on poor Sabine. The first move had to be to contact her and see if she would agree to talk to us. With no phone number, and nothing listed under her name in international directory enquiries, there remained little choice but to resort, again, to the laborious business of letter writing.

In our letter, we congratulated Sabine on having such a beautiful baby, and assured her that he was being well cared for. Not wanting to involve the authorities, there were a number of things we urgently needed to discuss with her. Would she be agreeable to meeting us, if we came to see her in Germany? We could make it the weekend after next, if convenient. Perhaps she could give us a ring.

The proposed date came and went, without a response. Undecided as to the best course of action, any new initiative was pre-empted by a phone call late one night. A tearful and near-incoherent Sabine announced herself. To me, the voice was that of a younger girl, rather than a mature woman. The conversation was difficult, partly because of Sabine's limited English but also due to her distressed condition.

She thanked us for our letter and asked after the baby. He was fine, we assured her, and being cared for by Rupert's aunt. Was Rupert himself there, she wanted to know, and sounded disappointed when told he wasn't and that we had no news of him.

Despite her poor command of the language, she made it quite clear from the outset that she did not want to meet us. On the other hand, she seemed loathe to break off the conversation - although I cannot recall every detail, the call lasted over half an hour. She certainly told me something about her situation and circumstances, and referred several times to the baby, at one point breaking down for nearly a minute. I'm no psychologist and could never make a counsellor but by the time she put the phone down I had won her agreement to a meeting in Krefeld just as soon as this could be arranged.

I cry a lot these days, since the breakdown. I can't help it, it just happens. All of a sudden my eyes fill with tears and it all comes out. I just sob uncontrollably. The doctor comes round once a week to check us over. The medicine doesn't agree with me, it makes me sick. I have told them, repeatedly, but they don't bloody listen or do anything about it. I'm really not at all well, you know.

I remember as a child getting chicken pox and spending weeks in bed with a raging temperature. There was this dream with bright flashing patterns, like the kaleidoscope which Tim and Sara had, and another one where I had to walk uphill up this road near home. But it was dark, like a tunnel, and I was frightened. Although I tried running, I could never reach the end. I've started getting these dreams again. I told Dr. Crapp last week but he just said it was interesting and left it at that. Crapp! That really is his name, if you can believe it!

And that's another thing. I have a problem with my stool. That's a word I've learnt here. I always thought a stool was what you sat on. You wouldn't want to sit on this sort. Golly no! Oh dear no. But that's something they really are interested in. I have to leave a 'specimen' which they take away for analysis. Rather them than me! They never tell me what it shows.

But I wouldn't want you to think that I only ever think about myself and my bodily problems, contemplating my navel, as it were. It's just that............

I have often wondered why I invariably fall prey to the first man who comes along and shows me some kindness; perhaps it runs in the family. At the age of 65, I had never expected my mother to re-marry, least of all someone 17 years her junior. The news came as a considerable shock.

She must have known I would disapprove, which was why I wasn't invited to the wedding. In fact, I was only told about it after the event. Richard had been a vague family friend, whom my parents had known through the Conservative Club. His own wife had died a few years previously, leaving him with a brood of five children, ranging in age from 12 to 30. The most successful was the eldest son, who had graduated from Cambridge with a First, and was Chief Accountant at the area gas board. By way of contrast, the youngest son had no formal qualifications at all, and was a manual labourer in a factory, making packaging materials.

The same enigmatic contrast was evident, also, in the father. Richard enjoyed an encyclopaedic knowledge, and had strongly held opinions, which brooked no argument, on subjects ranging from sport to politics; he was passionate about cricket. And yet he himself held a lowly and badly paid position as a warehouse tallyman, a job destined to be replaced by a computer. To me, his eyes always held a hint of madness and I had never felt comfortable in his company. His liking for children (he was also a school governor) also left me slightly uneasy.

All these emotions and more re-surfaced as I

travelled home to congratulate the newly weds. The atmosphere at Sunday lunch was strained, and it jarred to hear his twelve-year-old daughter call *my* mother Mum. Sixteen-year-old Jason sat glued to the television, a can of Special Brew clenched permanently in his hand.

Richard had thoughtfully brought with him the remnants of his litter still left at home, allegedly to help her with the cost of running the house. Meanwhile, he was supposed to be selling his own property. I couldn't honestly see any of them making much of a contribution, and wondered what value Richard's house might represent, after the mortgage was paid off. You couldn't help but question if he wasn't just an opportunist, and they were all sponging off a gullible old lady.

So it was with a sense of relief, that I boarded the train back to London that Sunday evening. It was hot in the carriage and, although I tried to focus on the problem of daddy bear and baby bear, it wasn't long before my head began to nod and fill with a sub-conscious stream of random images and disjointed thoughts.

Beck and I occupied a window seat like that on the train but, instead, on a cross-channel ferry. We sat very low in the water - our lower bodies and feet were, in effect, below water level. A constant parade of craft, from hydrofoils to bulk tankers, passed by, but all scaled down to the size of models. Gradually the sea rose, climbing above the window and, with a crazy logic, the water-borne craft turned into submarines, giant fish and aerodynamic trains. I woke as the water started to lap round my feet, only to discover that the heating in the carriage had failed, and an icy draught was trying to amputate my feet at the ankles.

Some days later, Beck and I were actually sitting on that submarine train, being whisked through the Tunnel. It wasn't just idle curiosity that was driving us to meet Sabine in her home town of Krefeld. It was essential that a solution be found to the problem of Baby, and quickly - the present situation just wasn't tenable. No, Sabine would have to accept the consequences of her actions and either take him back or arrange care. In this vein, we were developing quite an antipathy towards the person we had not yet even met. But, at the back of our minds, we cherished the secret hope, through Sabine, of finding Rupert.

It was already dark on our arrival in Krefeld and, unsure of our whereabouts, we jumped into a Mercedes taxi, handing the address to the driver on a slip of paper. Gladbacher Strasse was a busy thoroughfare, with trams running up a central reservation, and we had to strain to hear Sabine, through the intercom, inviting us up.

No. 61 was just one entrance of many along the grey concrete facade of what, in the post-war building boom, might have been considered a desirable apartment block. In the intervening years it had degenerated into little more than a rooming house, a status borne out by the heavy mixture of cooking smells on the staircase, the jumble of pushchairs and bikes on the landings, and the cacophony of sounds, emerging from behind the closed doors. Sabine's flat was on the top floor.

What met our gaze when the door swung open, came as something of a surprise. At first sight, we were faced with Sara's double, a genetic clone, but closer examination revealed essential differences. The dress, for example, would never have passed muster with the original Sara. The clone wore skin-tight leather trousers on what was, admittedly, a figure to be flaunted, a fact accentuated by the skimpy, bolero top. Eye-catching in a disco maybe, here at home it made the wearer look tarty, and the overall effect was finally destroyed by an incongruous pair of sandals. The face, too, didn't match up to Sara's model quality, Sabine in close-up proving coarse-featured and puffy, a fact partially concealed by a generous application of make-up.

But the greeting was warm, with none of the hysteria displayed in our initial telephone conversation. In fact, Sabine came across as mature beyond her years. Unless deceived, I put her age at no more than nineteen or twenty, which was confirmed later that evening. With a broad smile and manly handshake, she introduced herself with the single word "Schmitz", and made us welcome.

The flat was minute. From the tiny entrance hall, a door on the right opened onto a small bathroom and toilet, whilst straight ahead was the only other room which doubled up as kitchen, dining room, sitting room and bedroom. Beck and I were offered a seat on the divan, which was the only place to sit, except for two stools at a minute breakfast bar. Without formality, Sabine fetched three bottles of beer off the window ledge, thrust one each at Beck and myself and, squatting on a cushion on the floor, flipped the top off hers with her teeth. "*Prost*", she said with a boyish grin, waving the bottle in our direction before taking a long swig. Maybe Teutonic teeth are stronger than Anglo Saxon ones; be that as it may, neither Beck nor I was prepared to risk our molars for the sake of a macho, comradely gesture.

"*Ach so. Entschuldigung*. Sorry," Sabine apologised, correctly interpreting my bottle-opening mime. Standing up, she deftly prised the tops off both bottles on the door catch, before handing them back to us.

"*Prost*!" she volunteered again.

This time we responded in kind. "*Prost*!"

I felt we were going to get on.

I began to understand what Rupert had seen in Sabine, leaving aside the physical aspect. She had a natural warmth and robust, almost naive charm. Her personality immediately came across and, without any deliberate effort on her part, she successfully defused what could have been a difficult situation. She was a trainee in a bank, she explained, and had lived with her parents until meeting Rupert, and becoming pregnant. Her parents didn't know about the baby and would be very 'unfortunate' if they had found out. It'd been difficult keeping it from them, making excuses for not going home, and so on. But now everything was "OK".

Sabine didn't seem to fully grasp the situation.

"Sabine, we need to talk about the baby, OK?" I began. "He's a great little guy and we all love him to pieces." I put on what was meant to be a gooey look, only I could feel it start to go wrong. "But the thing is..... Let me put it this way - he needs a Mum, a real Mum. He needs *you*!"

Sabine looked blank. Beck took over.

"You haven't met Rupert's Aunt Mary, of course. She's a lovely lady, a real sweetie, and she loves the baby like he was her own. But Mary's already quite old. She'll be over seventy before he's even ten! Imagine! Don't misunderstand - she's perfectly happy looking after him but it'll become more and more of a strain as he grows up and she gets older. What's more, she doesn't have much money and couldn't possibly bring him up just on her pension. I guess it's different in Germany, but in our country you can barely clothe and feed yourself on the state pension, let alone raise a child. Anyway, the bottom line is .... that is to say, he needs you, both as his natural mother, and also to look after his material needs. So what do you say?"

Beck leant back, having said her piece. Sabine continued to look blank, saying nothing. For my part, I could feel the anger starting to rise in me, which Sabine clearly sensed, as a red flush began to spread up her neck.

Beck quickly stepped in: "Tell us about you and Rupert, Sabine. How did you come to meet?"

The answer to this, of course, we already knew.

It was on the beach in Spain, last year, she explained. She and her friend, Lisa, had been on holiday and got talking to the English boy one day. She liked him, and found it useful to practise her English, which she was taking at *Abitur*. Rupert, which she pronounced *Rrruepairt,* the 'R' spoken gutturally, came to see them every day. On one occasion, they were taken to meet a friend with whom he was staying, but the meeting wasn't a success. Apparently, Rupert was planning to come and work in Germany after the holiday. He'd been offered a place at the University of Cambridge, to study medicine, but couldn't take it up for a year and felt German might be useful in his studies. As he had no firm plans, Sabine suggested he came to Krefeld. If he wasn't averse to menial work, it should be possible to fix him up with some kind of job.

To cut a long story short, Rupert accompanied Sabine back to Krefeld and moved in with Rudi, a former boyfriend of hers, who had his own flat. It was there, in fact, that Baby Rupert was conceived.

The announcement of the pregnancy and Rudi's move to Berlin more or less coincided. Rupert, from the sound of it, took fright, and flight, on learning the news and was last seen heading east with Rudi.

It was in the telling of this story, that Sabine's stoicism showed the first cracks. I guessed that for her, our ursine friend had been more than just a passing holiday romance. His pretence and subsequent behaviour were, as we now knew, fully in character.

Three more beers were fetched from the window ledge and served in the same manner as before.

Another beer was the last thing I needed, and it didn't do much to quieten the rumbling of my stomach. What's more, it was getting late and we had nowhere to sleep. But Beck was anxious to learn more.

"Have you tried to contact Rupert? Do you know where he is? I've never been there but Berlin's a hell of a big place, isn't it?"

Sabine couldn't be sure exactly where they might be, but Rudi went to Berlin quite often on business, staying with friends in different places, sort of guest houses.

Closer questioning revealed that these so-called guest houses were in effect squats, situated in what had been East Berlin. Rudi himself sounded a dubious character, dealing in 'second-hand' cars and insurance write-offs, most of which found their way East. Rudi was the sort of person you read about.

Beck's supply of questions temporarily exhausted, her thoughts, like mine, turned to physical needs. World War Three was only averted, literally at the eleventh hour, when Sabine was finally persuaded to phone a *Pension* round the corner and book a double room for us. Prior to that, she was insisting we sleep at her place - a physical impossibility. We were quite glad to be left to our own devices - we needed to discuss our strategy before meeting her again next morning and were thankful too for an all-night snack bar which fixed us up with hamburger and chips, along with the inevitable beer.

"You say your parents would go ballistic if they found out, you know, go mad. OK, they may yell at you at first but, in my experience, they would soon come to terms with the situation and become doting grandparents before you know it. You'd be surprised. Something similar happened in our family. I know, believe me."

Beck had never told me this. I wondered if she was making it up. In any event, it cut no ice with our Sabine, who just kept shaking her head muttering "*Unmöglich*. Impossible."

Detecting that she was close to tears, and not wanting to provoke an emotional crisis, Beck beat a tactical retreat, leaving Sabine to dwell on a thinly disguised threat: "Of course, if you don't feel able to care for young Rupert yourself, you or your parents will have to make arrangements for a formal adoption. There are mechanisms for doing this - officially."

After a moment's delay: "I can give you an address. You can have the address," Sabine offered in panic.

"What sort of address? Which address?"

"You know, the Berlin house. I stayed there once with Rudi. I cannot write the complete post address but I can say you where it is."

"But if you know where to find them, why haven't you been there yourself, to talk to Rupert?"

"Rupert is no longer mine. He belong Rudi. I once too belong Rudi," with which Sabine pulled up her sleeve to reveal an inside arm, thick with tiny scars up to the elbow. As if to prove the point, the other sleeve too was rolled back, showing the same pock-marked pattern. "But now I no more belong him."

For me, the name Berlin had always held a fascination, a city razed to the ground, which then raised itself from the ashes, a conundrum evoking a host of contrasting images. The glitz and glamour of the West, epitomising the post-war *Wirtschaftswunder,* against the moral and physical impoverishment of the East, finally exposed to the eyes of the world by the removal of the Wall. A focal point in the Cold War - the airlift, Check Point Charlie, the building of the Wall, the stark images of bodies lying unattended in the glare of searchlights, Kennedy declaring himself a Berliner, the spy crossing a deserted bridge in the cold foggy night - the imagination could run riot.

In numbers, I have always found the Germans intimidating, but I warmed to them as the scenes of euphoria were beamed to the world, when East and West finally became re-united - ironically, not by diplomatic negotiation but as an inevitable consequence of a one-sided economic war. And this is only a part of the city's recent history, some of which I have experienced in my short lifetime. So the prospect of spending a brief holiday in Berlin, even a working one, came as no hardship. But it wasn't self-interest that led us to book a weekend trip, rather fear for the safety of a foolish young man for whom, despite everything, we still held a strong affection.

In finally volunteering an address of sorts for the two R's, Sabine had also offered to accompany us to Berlin. The offer was initially declined, for fear of provoking a negative reaction from Rupert, assuming, that is, he could actually be found. But after further reflection, we changed our minds in the hope that, together, we might more readily locate the squat.

On arrival, and although largely a stranger herself in Berlin, Sabine took matters in hand and ferried us onto the S-Bahn, heading off into what had been the Eastern Sector. The wealthy west was soon left behind, and we progressed through what is best described as a giant building site. Concrete tenement blocks, the pride of the Communist post-war era, were being demolished like stacks of cards to make way for new, low-rise apartment blocks, well-spaced with lawns, newly planted trees and children's play areas between. Gleaming shopping plazas with fountains and mirror-panelled office accommodation rose from the débris, whilst multi-lane highways left the few remaining pre-war, brick-built tenements isolated, like pre-historic tombs. It was to one of these, in a drab suburb, that we made our way.

Trams ground on uneven rails down the centre of the winding, cobbled street, and streams of cars constantly threatened to splash muddy water as they squeezed past in the gutter. The din of the traffic would have prevented us from hearing the intercom, even if it had been working, which I am sure it wasn't. But this didn't prevent Sabine from screaming into it with predictable results. It was hard to say from the outside whether or not the house was occupied. The rows of bell pushes, for the most part, still carried names, but these were faded and barely legible: Hartenberger, Olszewski, Braun, Holtkamp, Zellkoetter....... Metallic roller blinds guarded the downstairs windows, bearing an imaginative display of artistic graffiti. One blind had partially collapsed, revealing a grimy window, behind which hung a grey, tattered net curtain.

Undeterred, Sabine hammered with her fist on the front door, adding a few forceful kicks for good measure. After repeating this assault and waiting several minutes, a small flap opened in the door and the top half of a face appeared behind a grille. Following an exchange of words, the door was opened just sufficiently to allow us to squeeze through. The impact on the senses was immediate.

The smells which assailed the nostrils would have been an interesting subject for scientific analysis. The all-pervading odours of dampness, cooking, drains and general decay were easily identified. Overlying these were unfamiliar, sensation-inducing smells, not exactly incense, but nevertheless scented, sweet and bitter, cloying.

A dim, naked bulb hanging from the ceiling was the only source of light, making it difficult to examine closely the figure who had let us in. During a protracted conversation with Sabine, of which we understood very little, the sex was established as female, and the age similar to our own. Whilst not exactly stepping off the catwalk ourselves, we must have looked like supermodels in comparison. But putting appearance aside, the discussion seemed to be friendly enough, and resulted in our being ushered up to the first floor, negotiating holes in the stairs on the way.

There, in a large, high-ceilinged room at the rear of the house was gathered a motley assortment of humankind, lying on bare boards, and for the most part simply doing nothing. The glazed expressions, however, confirmed them as junkies, largely unaware of the world outside and the passing of time. The most coherent person seemed to be the girl who had let us in but the chances of gaining any helpful information from this bunch of zombies seemed remote. Nonetheless, further lengthy discussion followed, in German, in which the name of Rudi was mentioned many times, and Rupert once or twice. Beck and I felt both bored and uncomfortable at the same time, not least on account of the interest being shown in us by a shaven-headed character, who I could smell at ten paces. The rest hardly seemed aware of our presence. Just as we were beginning to wonder where to put ourselves, Sabine abruptly said: "OK, let's go," and led us downstairs where Cinders duly unbolted and unchained the door.

A grey day outside, the brightness was almost dazzling in contrast to the interior of the des-res we had just left, and the fume-laden air like nectar. A beer was mutually prescribed to wash away the after-taste of our visit, allowing Sabine the opportunity to report her findings. These were disappointing in the extreme. Rudi had gone East on one of his regular missions and wasn't expected back for some time. For his part, Rupert had left some time ago and hadn't been seen since. Baldy felt he may have moved on to Prague, where there was quite a scene, and offered to come with us. Someone else suggested we should visit some of the clubs where he had hung out - maybe some of his friends there knew where he was.

I don't suppose our middle-class parents would have approved of the accommodation Sabine arranged. The old witch, who responded to our summons on the bell, eyed us up and down and quoted two room rates - one for the night and one for the hour. We opted for the overnight rate and took a room with three beds. But the room was clean and functional, and thankfully faced the back. We shut our minds and ears to the comings and goings and sounds of the night.

Chez Mimi's window to the world was backed by a pink drape and displayed black-and-white photos of a number of unknown stars who, by implication, had performed at the club. The entrance was brightly lit by a spotlight, whilst the matt black door sported a circular one-way window and was firmly shut. One was conscious of being observed, having rung the bell to gain admission, and the door swiftly opened to usher us downstairs into the cellar. There, the heat and the stench of cheap perfume and Continental cigarettes were overpowering. These were generated by surprisingly few bodies, concentrated mainly round the bar, for which we also made a beeline, in the hope of finding someone who might know of Rupert and his whereabouts.

Most of those perched on the bar stools were heavily made-up women, predominantly blondes, with the odd punter interspersed. The gender of the bar person itself was indeterminate until Sabine pointed out that, as a gay bar, the barman would undoubtedly be a man in drag, as were the guests. I don't know about Beck, but at this revelation I felt myself go distinctly weak at the knees. My sheltered up-bringing hadn't prepared me for a place like this, and I had no desire to stay and see what developed.

The first beer cost the equivalent of £10 but included the floor show. I hadn't even noticed the dance area, which was later to be the setting for God knows what tawdry scenes of debauchery. That we emphatically did not want to see.

"Ach, but it can be really, really funny, completely crazy," Sabine assured us.

"Out of the question. *Unmöglich,*" we threw back at her, flaunting our newly acquired, if limited, German.

Disconcerted, Sabine addressed herself to the real matter in hand and made enquiries of the bar person. Much to my surprise, Rupert was not only known at Chez Mimi but had also worked behind the bar there. That said, he had not been seen for several months and, here too, nobody knew of his whereabouts. One of the 'girls' at the bar, introduced as Andrea and sporting a rather nasty shaving rash, asked to be remembered to Rupert - "Tell him, love from his bunny rabbit."

This seemed an appropriate time to leave, all the more so since, at that moment, a noisy party of well-oiled businessmen began to arrive.

"*Kommt*," said our leader, striding out. "We go where other."

Sabine's insistence almost caused an argument, she, determined to go on a club crawl, following up the leads provided at the squat, we, the English roses, demurring in favour of our beauty sleep. The truth was, we had a strong aversion to the sort of haunts apparently frequented by Rupert, not to mention the dubious company he kept. This wasn't the Rupert we had known, Sara's friend.

It was hard to get a word out of Sabine next day. Whilst she showed up for breakfast, it was only to drink a coffee, and her bed had not been slept in. She refused to say where she had been, or what she had been up to, and to describe her as taciturn would have been an exaggeration. Faced with leaving for London later that morning, the mood was one of despondency. Never strong, we had now completely lost the scent - the trail had gone cold and the prospect of traipsing round Europe, pursuing ever more slender clues, was not appealing. Not least, the problem of the baby demanded urgent resolution.

I'm feeling much better in myself these days, no more hallucinations, just the usual aches and pains. And I've started to put weight back on again, you'll be pleased to hear. They've stopped the injections too and started letting me go to the workshop. I'm making little place mats from straw and raffia. It's almost like being back at junior school. I may be able to go on to making stars and angels soon - as Christmas decorations, you know. If I need anything cutting I have to go to the supervisor. I sort of march up to him and snap to attention clicking my heels. It's just my little joke but we are not amused. He wears a uniform and has a dead-mouse moustache, you see.

But I still can't accept the things they do to you here - they're animals, the whole bloody, sadistic lot of them. Anyway, with any luck I shouldn't be here much longer.

I didn't kill her, you know - it was the horse that killed her. I don't know why I did it. On the other hand, she shouldn't have told me to pack my bags and leave - just because of her wanker of a boyfriend.

But it wasn't meant to happen the way it did. OK, Sara's horse was supposed to bolt but then I was going to catch it up and rein it in. Sara would be shaken but unhurt and I would be the hero of the hour. She would swoon into my arms promising to be mine for ever, just like in the movies. She couldn't possibly throw me out after that, could she, not after saving her life?

Yet it all went wrong. The horse overreacted - after all, I didn't jab it that hard. It should have just broken into a gallop. The chap at the stables must have known it was over-excitable - should never have hired her out, an unpredictable animal like that. I don't see how anyone could possibly blame me for what happened.

Tim understood, he's very understanding is Tim.

8

"I sent her packing, 'er from the Social," said Enid, "But I know she'll be back. Someone must have split."

An early visit to Great Langford had been a first priority, following the abortive trip to Berlin. We had manipulated Enid's emotions in leaving her with the baby and couldn't trade on her good nature indefinitely. Least of all she deserved some financial support; caring for the child would place an increasing burden on her. But we need not have worried about her mental attitude and she was clearly managing very well. We were welcomed with a warm hug, and from Baby a broad toothless grin. It was rewarding to see the changes in him in those few short weeks and we were sure he remembered us, until Enid pointed out that he smiled at everyone - he was such a happy baby and didn't appear to miss his real mother at all.

Enid's emotional attachment to the baby made it virtually impossible to discuss the practicalities of the situation with her. The prospect of losing him seemed to rob her of any rationale. But Baby's existence was now known to the authorities, and it could only be a matter of time before further enquiries were made, particularly as Enid had apparently been obstructive, if not rude.

As to the legalities, we were completely out of our depth. Professional advice was clearly needed and, by stretching our patience to the limits, we eventually succeeded in getting Enid to agree an approach to good old George Bulstrode. He, of all people, could surely be relied on to preserve confidentiality.

The leave-taking was quite emotional. We had to promise a tearful Enid to move heaven and earth to help her keep Baby. He for his part, untouched by the drama of the occasion, grinned like a lunatic and waved his little fists about in a frenzied sort of dance.

On our return, a missive was duly penned to dear George, signed of course by Beck. Before a reply was received, however, another completely unexpected letter dropped, like a bomb, through the door, this one bearing a Spanish stamp and post-marked Madrid. It fell to me to open it and read it first. It was from Quentin.

Madrid

Mesdames,

You are probably surprised to hear from me after so long. It may also come as something of a surprise if I tell you that I've vaguely kept in touch with Tim after you ran him to ground in Balduras. I think he would like to see you.

Please don't be shocked but you have to know what to expect. Tim is suffering from a wasting disease and has been in hospital here in Spain for several weeks. He is far from well now but is being cared for at home by Kevin who, despite everything, is coping magnificently. I hope you will be able to make it as he has especially asked for you.

I seem to be the bearer of nothing but bad tidings and have thought long and hard about whether, and how, to break this next piece of news to you or whether to leave it to Tim. You see Rupert is dead........

At this point my vision blurred and I had to sit down abruptly on the nearest chair. It took several minutes, with my head thrust inelegantly between my knees, before I was able to continue. In fact, the news was so shocking, I had to read the letter once more from the beginning to take it in.

.....Rupert is dead.

My eyes stopped again at this bald statement, and refused to go on, like a cursor on a computer screen that comes up against some invisible tab.

....Rupert is dead. I'm sorry to have to put it so bluntly but that's how Tim broke it to me. Sometimes it is the kindest way.

I think you know that Rupert went from Spain to Germany, ending up in Berlin. What exactly happened there I don't know - Tim wouldn't say, assuming he himself knows. Anyway, the foolish young man - I'm sorry, I shouldn't say that - got himself into trouble and Tim managed to get him repatriated back to Spain following some kind of financial settlement. It was not long after his return that he was tragically drowned in a swimming accident. Tim is quite desolé, as you can imagine. I assume you will want to see him and also visit the grave.

I wish I were writing to you in happier circumstances and would like to help in any way I can. Please look me up in Madrid if you would like to break your journey en route to Gerona.

With very best wishes

Your Quentin

I had read the letter twice more before Beck came home. I sat her down with a stiff gin and tonic before producing it. Like me, she was stunned by the news. Whilst we mulled over its contents till the small hours, and speculated over the possible circumstances of Rupert's tragic accident, there was nothing more to be extracted beyond the bare facts, as reported by Quentin. But two decisions were made – firstly, that the appalling news should be withheld from Enid and Sabine until all the facts were known and, secondly, that we would go to see Tim just as soon as the practical arrangements could be made.

And so it was, that two weeks later, we found ourselves re-visiting that corner of Spain we had first come to know in such different circumstances. The change was also reflected in the late November weather, which mirrored our sombre mood, Nature in harmony with Man. The heat of summer had been replaced by a grey sky and a chill dank wind, the holiday apartments abandoned and villas boarded up against the elements. The whole place seemed to have gone into hibernation. The few people and cars on the streets looked like the first survivors, crawling out of their bunkers after a nuclear holocaust. Even at Tim's place, the only sign of possible occupation was the rather battered, blue Fiat, standing outside, and that had a flat tyre. To all intents and purposes, the house was deserted.

But signs of life appeared after the second ring on the bell, and moments later the door was opened to reveal the figure of Kevin. Change too was written on the face of Tim's young friend who had matured disproportionately to the passage of time. Now in winter attire, he cut a more attractive figure and had allowed his hair to grow longer. The angry boil on his neck had disappeared to leave only a darker patch, and the remnants of teenage acne would soon be a thing of the past.

Kevin had also managed to acquire a certain presence and appeared more in control. It was hard to recognise him as the same awkward, inarticulate youth who had quivered under Tim's wrath on our last visit.

"Hi, you'd better come in here first," said Kevin, leading us into the living room. "Tim's asleep at the moment," he added, turning off the television, which was showing an old black-and-white American movie with Spanish sub-titles.

"Would you like a drink?" he offered.

Whilst Kevin was away preparing the coffee, we had time to examine our surroundings. The room was comfortably, if sparsely, furnished with reproduction traditional Spanish furniture. North African rugs added a touch of warmth to the otherwise bare, block-wood floor, whilst discreet lighting contributed to an overall effect of cosiness. Full-length sliding windows opened onto the patio and pool area, where we had first disturbed Tim, at his sunbathing. How long ago that seemed now.

The offer of a brandy to accompany the coffee was gratefully accepted. We felt tired after the journey and apprehensive about meeting Tim.

"How is he, Kevin?" we asked.

"He's not very well, really. In fact, he's not very well at all. But we're managing, you know."

Prompted by our questioning, Kevin went on to explain how he was coping with the practicalities of the situation. The more he spoke, the more impressed we became, and marvelled at the transformation that had taken place. Whilst the doctor visited once a week, home nursing help was virtually non-existent, and Kevin had had to learn skills, normally acquired only through professional training. His attention to the daily trivia of their existence showed a surprising organisational ability, and the way he spoke of Tim displayed a level of dedication and tenderness which were quite touching.

"You know its AIDS, don't you?" he said, confirming what we had all along suspected. "Full blown. It's just a matter of time now, I'm afraid." The voice began to break. Beck and I moved uncomfortably in our seats.

"He knows," followed by a deep intake of breath. "That's why he asked to see you, before it's too late." At this point Kevin covered his face with his raw-red hands to hide the tears, which began to flow uncontrollably. Beck waved me back into my chair as I started forward to comfort him. We waited in awkward silence until he was sufficiently recovered.

"Perhaps it'd be better if you came back tomorrow," he suggested. "He's having one of his bad days. In any case, I'm sure he'd prefer to tell you about Rupert himself. You could stay here, but you might have a rather disturbed night. There's the hotel in Balduras, the Splendida - you should be able to get in there at this time of the year, or have you already made a booking somewhere else?"

We hadn't, in fact, and accordingly headed off into the village in our rented car. The hotel we remembered seeing on our first visit, and found it without difficulty. Getting in was a different matter. Our fruitless efforts were witnessed by one of those ubiquitous, black-clad granny figures, who had been such a familiar sight on our previous visit. She gesticulated to us to ring on the house next door, which produced a surly, unshaven character who reluctantly let us in, and provided the key to room 21 on the upper floor. The room was drab, cold and cheerless, as well as utilitarian in the extreme. The naked 40 watt bulb was the only source of light and the tap dripped noisily into the tiny sink, half way up the wall. Thank God Beck had had the foresight to buy a bottle of brandy at the airport. A generous draught from this went some way to restoring the spirits, and it was in a somewhat improved frame of mind that we ventured forth in search of dinner.

If our digs were the pits, the restaurant was the tops. When abroad, Beck was prone to making comparisons with her own country, usually to the detriment of the same.

"Think what you get when you order a seafood platter at home, Phil," she pondered. "Straight out of the deep freeze and into the micro-wave. 'For best results, do not remove from packet and cook as instructed!' They wouldn't feed it to the cat here!" she fumed.

I wasn't too sure. Some of our fellow Europeans have a somewhat ambivalent attitude to the feline species. But the seafood platter was every bit as good as that we had eaten when last in Spain, and it took the best part of two hours to crack and pick our way through a mountain of crustaceans, accompanied by an excellent bottle of dry white wine. The meal was superb.

Relaxing with an espresso afterwards, we

pondered on what had been a long and eventful day. Kevin had confirmed what we had already suspected, namely that Tim's condition was indeed terminal and, from the sound of it, the illness more advanced than anticipated. We were not looking forward to our audience.

Even these premonitions didn't steel us sufficiently for the sight, which met our eyes when reverently shown into the sick room next day. What confronted us was a little old man, a wizened walnut, bearing little, if any, resemblance to the Tim we had met here before. Propped up in an upright armchair, Kevin had done his best to make Tim look normal. But the effect was nevertheless shocking. The blanket, wrapped round his legs, couldn't disguise their skeletal appearance, whilst the head had shrunk to little more than a skull with eyes. It was the eyes which struck me most, and which still haunt me, even now. They shone brightly, almost feverishly, out of hollow sockets, darting quickly to follow every movement, pick up each nuance. They burned into you like laser beams, reading your thoughts before you yourself became conscious of them. The mind too was focused, incisive. It was as though, sensing the approaching end, all the body's energies had been concentrated in the brain, mental adrenaline coursing into the cells. Vocal expression sometimes lagged behind, and Tim's condition dictated that the audience was frequently broken off. In all, it took three days before all could be told and, in the course of those three days, this person, whom we hardly knew, bared his soul to us, and what a tormented soul it was.

"I'm not a religious man," he began, "and I don't think I believe in God. I just pay lip service to the notion of His existence, since it's part of our culture, our social heritage. But if there is an after-life, then I shall surely burn in hell. And if there is such a thing as re-incarnation, I shall be the most lowly form of life on earth, an amorphous, primitive blob of matter, on which those one step up in the chain feed like leeches. And that would be more than I deserve."

The effort of this introduction, and the raw emotion behind the statement, brought on a fit of coughing which left Tim reaching for the oxygen mask. Kevin appeared at the door, hovering, but was impatiently waved away.

"But you really came to hear about Rupert, didn't you? You may already have gathered, that the Rupert you thought you knew was only one half of the real person. The real Rupert, sadly, was insecure, inadequate, and morally weak. He was a schizophrenic, living in a world of fantasy, a pathological liar. Without either myself or Sara as a prop, he was a nothing - like one of those toadstools that vanishes in a puff of dust. Having said all that, you'll probably find it all the more surprising if I tell you that, despite all his faults, despite everything he has done, I still love him!"

Tim paused to allow the gravity of this statement to sink in.

"I guess you've already pieced together quite a lot for yourselves. You've probably talked to Aunt Mary, so you know the family background, such as it is. I don't suppose you heard what happened after he walked out on his aunt though. That was the first time he'd been entirely on his own, no longer under our protection. The schizophrenia was already present, I suppose, in latent form. The role-playing, Rupert bear and that stuff, was a sublimated form. Anyway, after leaving Great Langford he went to Worcester, and what a disaster that turned out to be. He just couldn't cope - he was quite inadequate, you see - and simply went to pieces without us to keep an eye on him. Imagine, they found him lying on the grass by the river one day, stoned out of his mind. He was wearing a woman's dress, if you can believe it, and no underwear, skirt up over his head claiming he'd been raped. He was lucky to get away with a fine for that one.

"Then there was the so-called suicide attempt. That was just a trick to get hold of Sara, so she would take him under her wing - a piece of moral blackmail; that was quite obvious. Thank God it worked, though - there's no knowing what might have happened otherwise."

It wasn't until Rupert landed up in London, still in Sara's tow, that Tim came to see him again.

"Sara didn't know that Rupert and I were seeing each other in London. Perhaps it was just as well. When it came to Sara and me, Rupert was bi-sexual, you see. There's no question about my sexuality though," said Tim, with what would normally have passed as a rueful smile.

"I could see that things were becoming difficult for Sara, with him always around the place. He was getting to be an embarrassment to her, in more ways than one. She wanted to lead her own life, felt she'd propped him up long enough. You can understand that, can't you? Anyway, something clearly had to be done.

"I may have been a little economical with the truth when you came here before, for which I apologise. You see, our visit to Spain, Rupert's and mine, was planned some time before the funeral. I suggested it as a holiday at first, but if I'm honest I suppose I secretly hoped we might set up house together."

Things were starting to fall into place - the pre-booked flight ticket, for example. But why had Rupert pretended to be in Manchester, just ahead of that weekend? We asked Tim.

"It's quite simple, really. Rupert and I just needed a few days together in London. We needed to re-discover ourselves, to be sure of our ground. After all, it was a big move. Manchester was an innocent subterfuge, really, nothing more - didn't hurt anybody and it gave Sara a bit of a breathing space."

Now we understood why the relationship between Rupert and Sara had at times seemed strained during that weekend.

We wanted to know how Rupert had reacted to Sara's death. With the exception of the funeral, we hadn't seen him since the day of the accident.

With the perception of a media interviewer, Tim immediately interpreted the question for himself.

"I guess, what you're really asking is whether Rupert had any part in what happened. The answer has to be yes and no. That sounds a bit evasive, doesn't it?

"I can only draw my own conclusions from what he told me - after all, I wasn't there myself - and that's meant trying to reconcile a number of conflicting statements and comments. Some of them were downright lies, designed to help Rupert ingratiate himself with me. Others, I'm sure, were statements of fact and some were just the ramblings of a sick mind which has only now found peace.

"My own belief is that Sara's death *was* an accident, but provoked by Rupert's childish and irresponsible actions. He had conceived a scheme, a simple ruse. Had it worked, it would have elevated him in Sara's esteem, obliging her to find a permanent place for him in her life. At least, that was his perception, his scenario. But it went tragically wrong."

I wiped the palms of my hands with the handkerchief I had been clutching. Beck too was tense.

"The plan was, that with some assistance from Rupert, Sara's horse would bolt. He was a capable horseman and was confident he could overtake Sara and rein in the horse - in short, he would be the hero of the day. But you know better than I do what happened. You had the misfortune to be there and I am sincerely grateful to you for what you did."

Tim took a sip from a glass of water before continuing. His hand trembled.

"Rupert's attitude after the accident was ambivalent, to say the least, and I felt like killing him myself on more than one occasion. His only thoughts were for himself. He'd wanted to hurt and frighten Sara for what she was doing, and was angry that his plan had failed - that he couldn't perform the heroic deed. He wasn't sorry she'd been killed, not really. What you saw at the funeral was only acting - him trying to mirror my sentiments, because that was what he thought I would want. You see, he was on his own then, wasn't he? He needed me. It didn't matter that he would have dropped me like a stone if his pathetic little scheme had worked. But it hadn't, so now he needed me."

Tim's breathing had become rapid and shallow. We were concerned that the excitement might lead to hyper-ventilation, and summoned Kevin who calmly administered more of the magical oxygen from the ugly cylinder, next to the chair. But the benefit was only short-lived and failed to halt the deterioration in his condition.

"Perhaps you could come back tomorrow," suggested the solicitous Kevin. "He's really had enough for one day."

What we had been told about Rupert had come as no real surprise and, whilst it had initially been our self-imposed remit to investigate that tragic accident on Bredon Hill, it no longer seemed important, not in the light of subsequent events.

With some hours of daylight still left, we decided to use the time in seeking out Rupert's grave. Outside, the sky was still heavily overcast and the chill wind from the east had, if anything, picked up in strength. What we assumed to be the only cemetery, we had passed on the road to Figueres on our previous visit. Standing on a barren hillside, it was surrounded by a high, stone wall, above which protruded a group of slender cypresses. The huge and ornate wrought-iron gates were open and, leaving the car outside, we set off up the gravel path.

Those graves closest to the entrance and towards the centre were larger and more ostentatious, some marked by tall, iron crosses, many incorporating faded, black-and-white photographs of the occupants. Here and there, a candle burned in its red glass container and quantities of flowers bore witness to the last visit of the mourners. The grandest monuments to the dead were imposing, stone-built mausoleums, reserved for whole families and generations.

Rupert's grave, in contrast, was modest in the extreme and bore no flowers, only an empty, cracked alabaster vase. It took some little time to locate, being situated amongst other more recently dug graves in a remote corner, clearly reserved for the poor of the community. Marked by simple wooden crosses with the name and dates carved or burnt into the wood, some bore the trade or craft of the dead, as though to enhance their status. Rupert's had a low headstone, simply bearing the name Rupert

Cunningham and the date of death. No date of birth, no epitaph, no prayer, no message of comfort or hope, the absence itself a commentary on the empty life of a confused soul.

Side by side, we stood before the grave, in silence.

It now seemed like years since we'd embarked on the search for a close friend, a friend who, for whatever reason, had abruptly disappeared from our lives. Through him, we had hoped to learn the truth about Sara's premature death. The hunt had ended here, on a barren hillside in Spain, and in tracking Rupert to his grave, the true circumstances of the accident had indeed been uncovered. But there was no sense of achievement, just an overwhelming emptiness. It wasn't meant to end like this; better we hadn't discovered the real Rupert, but continued to live in ignorance and enjoy the cherished memory of Rupert the Bear.

No tears were shed, no flowers laid or words spoken. It was eventually the cold which, by mutual consent, led us to turn away and make tracks for the meagre comfort of our hotel.

Tim was still in bed asleep, as we entered the bedroom next morning. The smell of the sick room assaulted the nostrils in a way it hadn't the day before. In contrast to the living room, the furnishings here were, at first glance, opulent but closer examination showed them to be cheap imitations, an attempt to replicate the grander life-style of a former age. The effect was vulgar.

Tim stirred without opening his eyes and retched feebly. A thin stream of green bile spilled from his mouth onto the sheet. The ever-watchful Kevin, sensing the situation, appeared as if by magic, and cleaned him up. Beck and I sat and waited until he felt able to carry on where he had left off the day before.

"You're probably wanting to know exactly what happened to Rupert, how he drowned. Am I right?"

The question intended rhetorically, there was no pause for an answer.

"Well, Rupert spent most of his time down on the beach, you know, the nudist beach. I don't know what it's called locally - I suppose it has a name. Anyway, it doesn't matter. Some evenings he would go there for a swim after dinner, which is what he did six weeks ago. And never came back. It looks perfectly safe for swimming but it has quite a reputation in the area. You only learn this afterwards, of course. One day you can swim out miles, and still put your feet down. Next day, in exactly the same spot, there'll be a channel with a strong undercurrent which can literally pull you under. People are tempted into the water because it's still relatively warm but it was really too late in the season to be bathing. Anyway, we alerted the police next day when we discovered he hadn't returned."

Tim drew in his breath sharply at this point and shuddered, as he exhaled.

"They found him three weeks later, washed up

twenty miles along the coast. I had to identify the body. I can't begin to describe......."

It took some minutes before Tim had composed himself sufficiently to continue.

"He hadn't been back very long, you know, from Berlin. He hadn't really settled. It was almost as though he'd lost his way somehow, was trying to find himself. Oh, the whole business was so desperately sad."

Again, a pause for what seemed like minutes.

"Did you ever manage to find him in Germany?"

It was now our turn to fill in some gaps for Tim. The meeting with Sabine in Krefeld was recounted and the subsequent trip to Berlin. Details of the night-club and Rupert's apparent life-style were deliberately omitted. We spoke about the baby and how he was such a little charmer, just like his father had been. This last brought a frown to Tim's brow and it was only then we realised he knew nothing of Baby Rupert's existence. The news affected him deeply. We explained the dilemma over Baby's future and the situation with Enid, about how a solution must be found, and soon.

Tim struggled to speak. "Don't w-worry about the financial aspect," he finally managed. "I'll look after all that side of things. But I think you ought to arrange for a blood test, you know, in view of the - er - circumstances."

This was doubtless sound advice, but it was nevertheless shocking to think that this innocent, young soul might have to suffer for the transgressions of its elders.

This was the last coherent sentence that Tim managed to utter that day. The remainder of the session became disjointed, to the point where it had to be abandoned. He appeared to be wrestling with some inner torment, but whenever he tried to express himself, bring whatever it was to the surface, he simply closed his eyes and seemingly fell asleep. For our part, we had reached an emotional vacuum. Spain no longer held anything for us, our place was back in England where lives had to be led and plans laid. But whenever we tried to take our leave, Tim became agitated, almost animated, to the point where we eventually agreed to make one last visit the following day.

"Gloria's death wasn't an accident!"

Tim was propped up in the armchair, as on the first day. He had clearly been bracing himself for this moment for hours, and we barely had time to sit down before he dropped his bombshell. The pause that followed was not for dramatic effect.

"I engineered it. What does that make me in the eyes of the law?"

Tim doubtless realised the irrelevance of the law in his particular case and the irony of the question.

"My punishment is being meted out now, through natural justice. It doesn't need the hand of man. No human punishment could be worse than this.

"She'd never been a good mother to us, you know. She thought only of herself. It was her fault the marriage broke down and we were the ones who had to suffer, without a father. She disgusted me, with her drinking and her ridiculous appearance - even at school the other kids would make jokes about her. We were ashamed of our own mother - imagine!

"The village people only tolerated her because she lived in a big house and they thought she had money. *And* she was going to pieces - it was only a matter of time before she would have to be looked after and I didn't see why either Sara or I should ruin our lives for the sake of someone who couldn't even be bothered to look after her own children.

"But having said all that, there's absolutely no justification for what I did. It was quite inexcusable and utterly despicable - and I didn't even have the bottle, the moral courage, to do the dirty deed myself.

"The mechanics of it were so easy you wouldn't believe it. I just made enquiries at one of the clubs, was introduced to two guys and paid them £1000 up front with the rest on completion. A straight-forward clinical deal."

The confession too was made in an equally clinical, dispassionate manner, with none of the raw emotion shown when talking of Rupert. Beck and I sat spellbound, horrified.

"But I did draw the line at violence. They wanted to break in, and literally club her to death, make it look like a burglary gone wrong. It happens all the time, unplanned crimes committed for petty sums to feed drug habits, you know the sort of thing. But that's not what I wanted and I insisted they did it my way. Yes, they did have to knock her unconscious, but I guess they never found the bruise in the autopsy or, if they did, they reckoned she hit her head as she fell.

"I'd worked out that they might come after me for more money, especially if they discovered I was in line for a big inheritance. That was one of the reasons for coming to Spain in the first place. In fact, they didn't even wait that long and I had to give them another £2000 before I could settle my affairs and get out.

"Sara knew nothing of all this, I really want you to believe that. She may have been a bit dizzy but she lived on a higher ethical plane. I could never have told her what happened and I wouldn't be telling you now if she were still alive.

"In fact, why am I telling you at all? After all, I could have taken the secret with me to my grave. It's not fair on you and you really must be very shocked - I'm sorry. I suppose I'm trying, in a way, to shed some of the guilt, for purely selfish motives. You must think me despicable."

Before we could respond, Tim's body again switched to defensive mode and the breathing became laboured. He was right. We were shocked and yes, we did consider him despicable, beneath contempt. We didn't want to know all this stuff and rued the decision to come to Spain, to answer the summons. It was impossible to sit and watch him any longer, the mask clamped over his wretched face.

“Do you think we could have a drink please, Kevin, something strong?” Beck asked, following a retreat to the kitchen where Kevin was preparing food.

“Sure, sure,” he said, unquestioningly. “Should have asked if you wanted anything earlier. Brandy OK?”

Sitting at the kitchen table clasping our brandy, we followed Kevin’s movements, wondering how much, if anything, he knew of all this. Tim’s friend possessed no great intellect, neither had he displayed any acting skills on our first encounter. We couldn’t imagine him being devious and concluded that he was as much in the dark as we had been an hour earlier. At what point had Tim picked him up and what was his background? Whatever, Tim had good cause to be deeply grateful to him now.

My first instinct, after the brandy, was to walk out and catch the next flight back to London. It was Beck who persuaded me to go back into Tim’s boudoir and hear him out, but it took a second drink, before I could summon up the courage. The stuffy smell of the sick-room was nauseating now and I tried to take shallow breaths, so as not to fill my lungs with the stale air.

Tim had been crying and was barely in control.

“I guess you just want to get the hell out of here,” he said, reading our thoughts perfectly. “But I have one last request - I need to make a will.

“All the papers relating to this property and my

assets are in this envelope. There's also a note detailing my bequests. I'm leaving something to Kevin, as a token of my gratitude, and to help him build a new life. I have also added a not insignificant sum to be held in trust for Rupert's son - it can be administered as required by the solicitor as trustee. Your kindness in coming here and, I hope, in arranging the will is also rewarded. The balance, which represents the majority of the estate, I shall be giving to AIDS research. The fact that I'm dying from AIDS could be seen as divine retribution. For many like me, though, it's the deadly penalty for being born with the wrong genes.

"I know you despise me and wouldn't expect otherwise. But I hope your generosity of spirit can overcome your emotions. I would be extremely grateful if you could take the envelope and give it to our old family solicitor in Hereford. It is addressed but I'd appreciate it if you could deliver it in person. George is a good chap and will do whatever is necessary. Once he has drawn up the will, it should be sent here, where I'll arrange for a notary public to witness my signature.

"I haven't got much time left, so please don't delay. Kevin has an adequate supply of morphine, and once the will is settled he'll help me through. You don't need to get involved in any of the practical arrangements - he knows what to do."

Tim closed his eyes and sighed. Without opening them again, he said "Goodbye, and thank you. Please don't pray for me."

We couldn't bring ourselves to touch him.

Hereford

My dear Rebecca,

So nice to hear from you again. My own knowledge of adoption etc. is somewhat limited. I would ideally like to consult one of our partners, Angela Cartwright, who specialises in this area, but she is unfortunately absent on maternity leave.

As I understand it, there is no reason why Enid Carter should not apply for adoption. The fact of her age and that she is single would not technically preclude consideration of an application. The permission of the blood parent(s) would be required but I gather that should not be a problem in this case, since you have access to the mother and she herself does not want to care for the child. On the other hand, factors such as the discrepancy between Mrs. Carter's age and that of the child would certainly be taken into account. The authorities can be quite sniffy in these matters.

But I really wonder, from what you have told me, whether an application for adoption would be the most appropriate course of action. The mother, I gather, is still quite young, although legally no longer a minor. She may, at some future date wish to care for the child herself - people are prone to mood swings and you cannot rule out the possibility that her actions were a consequence of post-natal depression, which nowadays is recognised as a medical condition. Equally, her rejection of the child may have been simply a short-term reaction to the departure of the father. The emotions can be quite a minefield.

All things considered, my advice to you would be to allow things to carry on as they are for a while and, after a suitable interval, try again to persuade the mother to take back the child. In the long term, however, it may be quite possible for Mrs. Carter to act as guardian, with the mother's consent, without going through formal adoption procedures. Mrs. Carter is, after all, a blood relative of the child. But I would need to seek an opinion from Angela once she is back in circulation. In any event, I think it most wise to obtain documentary evidence of the fact that the child is being cared for with the full knowledge and agreement of Fräulein Schmitz.

I hope these comments will be of some help to you. You may like to consult Angela together with Mrs. Carter when she returns in about two months' time. It goes without saying that I would be delighted to meet you socially at any time if your travels again take you this way.

With all best wishes,

George

Beck phoned George from work to thank him for his letter and tell him about our latest visit to Spain. He offered his condolences on Rupert's death and, despite Tim's specific request, saw no necessity for the papers to be delivered in person. It would be quite sufficient to send them by recorded delivery, which she should do without delay in view of the circumstances. For our peace of mind, he would acknowledge receipt and promised to deal with the matter straight away. Beck also thanked him for his advice on the baby situation, which was gladly accepted, not least because it deferred making a difficult decision. In any event, we would have to visit Enid again soon in order to break the shocking news about Rupert - not a task we were relishing.

In phoning George, it had been decided not, at this stage, to disclose details of Tim's confession. Tim, it was reasoned, was the only person with knowledge of the murderers. From his account, it was highly doubtful if they could be identified, still less brought to book. Even if that were possible, Tim's evidence would be crucial to the prosecution and there was no guarantee he would co-operate. After all, to do so would mean condemning himself at the same time. Either way, he would be dead long before the case ever came before the courts. The question effectively answered itself - silence was the only practical option. Tim had burdened us with a secret, which would have to stay bottled up for the rest of our lives.

It was only later, that the enormity of the moral and practical dilemma posed by Tim's disclosures came home to us. A murder had been committed, to which he was an accessory, even more, of which he was the instigator. In handling the papers, we were knowingly assisting in the dispersal of assets gained as a direct consequence of the crime. Not only that, we were to be beneficiaries under the will - we stood to gain from that very crime! Like it or not, we were in it up to the hilt.

Yet if we went to the police at this late stage, our own actions might be construed in a very unfavourable light. It could be argued that we had been a party to the crime all along, that the legacy was, in effect, hush money. And our reason for reporting the matter now? - Pangs of conscience? A dispute over the amount we were promised and a need to exact revenge? Panic? There was no shortage of plausible explanations which could be found and none of them left us looking whiter than white. God, had we been naive, simply doing nothing, taking what we thought was a practical approach to the problem, in the hope that it would just go away. No, there was no obvious way out of this mess.

The letter to Sabine posed less of a problem and was easily despatched. The other piece of unfinished business, however, promised to be less straight-forward but couldn't be deferred.

Number 11 Prospect Terrace boasted home-made paper chains in the front window in celebration of the approaching festive season. But whilst bearing goodwill, we certainly didn't bring any festive cheer. Enid read at once, from our faces, that something was wrong. Foregoing the usual courtesies, she sat us down and demanded to know what the matter was. We chose our words carefully, in breaking the news of Rupert's death - they had been rehearsed many times. Surprisingly, Enid didn't seem too shocked and displayed little emotion - in fact, she seemed almost relieved.

"I thought at first you'd come with some bad news about the baby, you know, to say they were going to take him away. Yes, of course it's very sad about Brian, but I always knew he'd come to a sticky end, from the day he walked out of here."

Although she spoke at length about Rupert, Enid's main pre-occupation was the baby. Nothing further had been heard from 'the Social', and George's advice was readily accepted. It was quite clear she wanted us to obtain Sabine's agreement to her looking after the baby, at least for the time being. This we undertook to do, but not without some misgivings - Sabine had so far failed to respond to our letter, breaking the news about Rupert.

Before leaving, we were allowed to see Baby who was enjoying his afternoon nap. Beck visibly melted at the sight of him, leaving herself open to accusations of broodiness on the way back. But I know how she felt.

Back at base, and despite our problems, we enjoyed a welcome, if temporary, breathing space and tried to focus once more on our sadly neglected social lives. Since the Randy disaster and Beck's equally catastrophic adventure with her married fella, we had both been virtuously celibate, though Beck maintained that for her, intercourse of the social kind could be equally as satisfying as the sexual variety. Sad cow.

Geoff, one of our more junior account managers at work, had been taking an interest in me for some time and had invited me for a drink, after work, on more than one occasion. For perfectly valid reasons, I had been obliged, each time, to decline until he finally gave up asking. As far as I knew, he was single and, like me, without any ties. To look at, he wasn't exactly God's gift, but then neither am I. In our limited dealings at work, he had treated me as an equal, and I had felt relaxed with him. I was sure we could enjoy each other's company without any pressures and accordingly let it be known that, should a further invitation be forthcoming, there was every possibility it would be accepted, which it did and was.

The trysting place was the Prince Albert, round the corner from work, which as a subject was studiously avoided. Instead, the conversation, which flowed easily, centred on each other, a real getting-to-know-you session. And what I got to know of Geoff was not displeasing and I think his impression of me was the same. Contrary to expectations, he shared my dry, possibly cynical, sense of humour, if such it can be called, and was also an exile in the metropolis, hailing originally from Chester. His sport was badminton and he was also a keen follower of rugby, not to mention enjoying an interest in classical music. The flat he occupied in

Battersea was shared with two others, both old university friends from Durham.

Whilst we hit it off pretty well at this first meeting, I was determined not to rush into any new relationship, repeating past mistakes. If something more than friendship developed, it would have to take its natural course. I think Geoff understood perfectly when, after two hours, I politely thanked him and said goodbye, hoping we could meet again for another drink soon. The hope was fulfilled, in fact several times, over the next few weeks, followed by a dinner date and a concert. The relationship grew naturally and with increasing intimacy, but stopping short of any direct sexual contact.

I was again enjoying life and starting to make up for all the time and energy lost in pursuing Rupert. Thanks to a greater focus on work too, my efforts were being rewarded and another promotion was in prospect. This time, I would be at the sharp end, part of a presentational team - and the job carried a company car. New horizons beckoned.

But the Black Cloud still hung over us. And a lot of midnight oil was burned, as Beck and I huddled round the fire, night after night, wrestling with the problem. George had to be told. He should have been told straight away. Under no circumstances could we accept the money. We simply had to go to the police. The longer we delayed............

It was on one such night that there was a ring on the doorbell. We both looked at each other, expectantly. Double glazing, a copy of the

Watchtower, a free carpet shampoo? A bit late for that really. Clearly, neither expected a visitor and neither was competing for the privilege of answering the door. With a martyr's sigh, I finally heaved myself out of the chair.

The figure, silhouetted against the frosted glass by the street lamp, looked vaguely familiar but I still opened the door with caution, and then only a crack.

"Any room at the old albergo?" it said. "It's colder than a witch's tit out here."

9

"Rupert, you're dead!"

"So *that's* why I'm surrounded by such heavenly creatures. And I never thought I'd make it. Ha-ha!"

"Cut the crap, Rupert!" Beck the Rottweiler - this was out of character. I was amazed. "You've got some explaining to do, so let's have it - *now*."

Her tone, as much as the words, had an immediate impact on Rupert. He turned pale, visibly shaken. This wasn't the Beck he knew, nor the welcome he had expected.

Since our last encounter, he had become more stocky and lost something of his youthful complexion. His hair was thinning at the crown and the attempt at growing a beard was an abject failure - the ginger fuzz did nothing to enhance his masculinity. But it was the eyes, constantly shifting, which betrayed a restlessness and deeper insecurity.

"Well, perhaps I haven't quite played the white man, always kept a straight bat and all that but.......," he trailed off.

Beck and I remained stony-faced, saying nothing. Even thick-skinned Rupert could sense the aggression - the air was charged with it. I swear that if he'd got the next move wrong, we'd have torn him limb from limb and fed him to the dogs, not that we had any.

"I only need somewhere to stay, just for a day or two - until I sort myself out," he whined. "After all, we are still friends, aren't we? I mean, we've been through a lot together, had some jolly good times, too, and cracked a few bottles?" Rupert introduced a questioning inflexion into his voice in the hope of getting us to agree.

We almost took a sadistic pleasure in watching him visibly deflate. What Tim had said was true - he *was* weak and it had taken very little to strip away the facade. We already knew what lay underneath and no longer found it attractive. What we really wanted to know was the truth. What really had happened and whose body was it in the grave in Spain?

"Talk, Rupert. Just talk!"

And talk he did. This, abridged, is the Bear's Tale:

"I don't know why Sara's horse took off like that, like an Exocet bloody missile. Huh, more like a Scud, I suppose. It certainly went off course, didn't it? It was nothing I did. In fact, I felt really rotten about the whole thing afterwards, as though it was somehow my fault. That's why I couldn't bring myself to speak to you both. You probably felt I should've stopped the wretched thing. If anything, I blame the chap who hired it out - he *must* have known how temperamental it was, he just *must* have.

“You probably don’t know this, but Sara had asked me to marry her and I’d agreed. It was after we all went to bed - after your famous dinner in the cottage, Phil. I know what you’re thinking. It should’ve been me asking Sara - after all, it wasn’t a leap year or anything. But you know what she was like, very strong-willed. I guess it’d been on the cards for some time - we were very close, you know. But I’d waited, hoping she’d suggest it first. Then I could be sure she really meant it. Can you understand that?

“That made it all the worse when she...........I’m sorry about this.

“Tim was an absolute brick. I reckon he saved my bacon, getting me to come to Spain. He could see what I couldn’t - that it’d be far too painful to carry on living in London, with all those memories. I really don’t know what I would have done without him.

“Spain was brilliant and Tim’s place just fantastic, just a few minutes walk to the beach. We had some terrific times, wall-to-bloody-wall sunshine, smashing food, even a bit of nooky. I sent you a card, didn’t I? Hope you got it. Good egg.

“But all good things must come to an end, time to move on and all that. So I got myself a couple of part-time jobs and took a room, not far away, so I could keep in touch with Tim. He could lead his life and me mine. If he wanted me or needed me, he only had to shout.

“You don’t need much to live on out there, you know. But the big thing was, I could concentrate on my real work - you know, writing my thesis - before taking up the place at Cambridge. That's why I've come back, you see - to take up this place they've offered me. But that's a few weeks off yet. That's why I need somewhere to stay for a bit. So what do you say?"

We were at a loss for words after this amazing narrative but it was already after one o'clock, with work for both of us in the morning. We couldn't throw Rupert out into the night but under no circumstances were we going to allow him to move in.

"Well, you've certainly seen a bit of life since we last saw you, Rupert. I don't know about Beck, but there are one or two things you might be able to help me with. But we'd better leave that till tomorrow. You're welcome to crash out on the floor for tonight but there's no way we can put you up for any length of time. As you can see, we just don't have the room. OK?"

Rupert nodded in gratitude, clearly relieved, and set about making himself at home on the floor of our sitting room. In saying goodnight to Beck, and out of earshot from our homeless house guest, I managed to whisper a few words of advice: "Keep your valuables under lock and key as long as he's staying here. Know what I mean?"

"Don't you think you're forgetting something?" I asked.

Rupert shrugged, looking perplexed.

“Doesn’t the word *Germany* mean anything to you?” said Beck with heavy emphasis.

“Should it?” he queried, still puzzled.

It was the day after Rupert’s dramatic re-appearance. We had been greeted on our return from work that evening by an appetising smell of cooking.

“Can’t beat a good spag. bol.,” Rupert had maintained, appearing at the kitchen door wearing my Charles and Diana wedding apron, a birthday gift from my mother. “Be ready soon.”

Beck and I had looked at each other, eyebrows raised in surprise.

“Smells great, Rupert, but you really shouldn’t have gone to all this trouble. We don’t normally bother much of an evening.”

It was after the bottle of Bulgarian country wine, also provided by Rupert, that we pursued our interrogation.

“Germany? Krefeld? Berlin? Of course it should mean something to you. It did to Sabine - and Spain did too! Come on, Rupert. We’re not bloody stupid, you know, so *stop* messing us about.” I was red in the face and getting angry now.

“Come on old chap, spill the beans,” mocked Beck, doing one of her nauseating male impersonations. “Can’t keep stumm any longer.” She winked at me, concerned about my blood pressure.

“Yes, I suppose I did go to Germany for a bit, working my passage, so to speak. There’s nothing wrong in that, is there? I mean, what is there to get so steamed up about? I don't understand your problem, Phil."

"I don't have a problem as such - only indirectly. And I have no problem with you going to Germany. Where I *do* have a problem is with you only telling us half-truths, not to mention the downright lies. We already know most of the story, *Mr. White*, and are quite capable of piecing together the rest for ourselves, but we'd rather hear it from the horse's mouth. And from what we do know, *B-rian*, you are in deep shit, deep deep shit. So do *not*, repeat *do not* fuck us about!" I was near hysterical by this time.

"Phil, a word in your shell-like, if I may, my dear," said Beck, almost forcibly marching me out to the kitchen.

"For Christ's sake, calm down. This isn't going to get us anywhere. He'll just clam up completely if we're not careful. Look, we're not going to find out any more about the riding accident, are we? I think Tim got it just about right, only Rupert isn't going to admit it. What we really need to know is what happened after he returned to Spain - you know, like whose body is it, who did they bury? And why? And what does he propose to do about his son?"

"Well, I think we're wasting our time with this guy. He's living on another planet and I can't take any more of this shit."

"You may well be right, Phil, but you're going to self-destruct if you don't take a grip. Let's try another tack. Bring in that bottle of Chardonnay from the fridge."

"In your place, I would be really proud, you know."

"Why, what do you mean?" asked Rupert, interested.

"Well, he's such a little smasher. And he looks just like his dad."

Beck sat back, waiting for a response. It took a few moments in coming.

"Yes, a great little chap." said Rupert, hesitantly.

I had the distinct impression that he knew less of his son's existence than we gave him credit for.

"You've - um - seen him recently then?"

It would have been cruel to play him along any further.

"Sabine had a little boy and called him after you - er, Rupert, that is. He's living with your aunt in Great Langford. She loves him to pieces, we all do, in fact. You will too....assuming you haven't already seen him."

Rupert just nodded. He seemed quite humbled.

"That's one of our problems, you see, Rupert. We need to discuss his future, make some plans. Tim was planning to leave some money for him in trust. We assume the will was drawn up and everything, so that should all be taken care of. Have you had any news of Tim? Do you know how he's getting on?"

Rupert's head hung such that it was impossible to see his face. The grunt was almost inaudible, the shake of the head required no interpretation.

"What exactly happened after Berlin?" Beck asked gently, the gravity of the question barely apparent.

Rupert, head still lowered, began to speak, coherently albeit in a monotone. Things hadn't worked out in Berlin. He'd got into a spot of bother which had taken a while to sort out. Tim had finally arranged things such that he could return to Balduras and live under his roof there, something for which he was genuinely grateful.

Tim had never been particularly well during the time Rupert had known him in Spain, and had suffered a number of seemingly unrelated illnesses, which had left him more and more debilitated. It was Rupert and Kevin, in fact, who had finally persuaded Tim to consult a doctor and undergo a series of tests. Tim was diagnosed as HIV positive.

By his own admission, Rupert was a coward when it came to facing up to unpleasant situations. As Tim's condition began to deteriorate, Rupert could not bear to see his friend suffer and took the coward's way out. He ran away.

He managed to hang on in Spain for a couple of months, just bumming around, as he put it. It was finally his dwindling financial reserves, which compelled him to return to England and present himself on our doorstep.

Even at the end of this monologue, Rupert still couldn't bring himself to raise his head and look us in the eye. The ensuing silence didn't seem to embarrass him and it was finally left to Beck to break the vacuum.

"Here, Rupert," she said, introducing a glass of wine into his field of vision.

"Thanks," he mumbled, taking the glass and lifting his head to take a sip. In doing so, his eyes passed across our faces and quickly dropped again. For a long time nobody spoke. Again, it was Beck who broke the silence.

"I can understand you being unable to handle the Tim situation. Not everyone can come to terms with a thing like that and we do sympathise. But there's one thing that's still bugging me. In Spain we were told you'd died; we even found your grave. If you're here, Rupert, who's grave is it?"

"Don't know, can't help you there," came the muttered reply.

"Tim said you'd drowned in a swimming accident. He even identified the body himself, your body."

"Really can't help you. Sorry."

Watching this exchange, I felt certain Rupert was lying, but how to get to the truth? I decided to try another approach.

"After the accident, Rupert, there was a major investigation into Sara's death. One of the theories was that you were somehow involved in what happened. The police asked us a lot of questions and also wanted to know where you could be found. They also asked about your attitude towards Gloria. Of course, we couldn't help them at the time - we didn't know where you were ourselves. Now you're back, of course, the situation has changed rather........What I mean is, Rupert........I know I lost my rag a bit back there, but I just want you to know that we are still friends after all, and if there is anything we can do to help, you know......"

Rupert at last raised his head and looked me in the eye.

"Thanks, Phil," he said, genuinely grateful. "Thanks."

The tactic didn't seem to have worked.

"That's OK," I said warmly. "What are friends for?"

God, I loathed myself for this sickening performance. I would be challenging Beck for the Oscar soon.

"We reckoned at the time that the police knew more than they let on. They were still asking questions, even after the inquest. If Gloria's death was suspicious, if for example she had been murdered, they probably felt they were more likely to catch the assassins off guard *after* the inquest.

"They say that Gloria suffered a blow to the head. The coroner concluded that she struck it after being overcome by the gas. But supposing she'd been hit on the head deliberately, by a third party who had then turned on the gas before leaving. In other words a *murder.*"

"Yes, but who would have a motive?" asked Beck, right on cue. "Nothing was taken, was it, and the only person to benefit was Tim - under the will. There's no way he could have raised a hand against his own mother. But the way he disappeared after the funeral.......But then, so did you, didn't you Rupert?"

Perspiration stood out on Rupert's brow. He wiped his hands nervously on his trousers and looked about to say something but stopped. Beck and I sat staring at him, saying nothing. He swallowed hard, several times, as if fighting back a rising tide of nausea.

"The body......," Rupert finally managed, "The body.......it was one of them, the hit men! They came after Tim, demanding more money. Christ knows how they traced him there, but they did. I had no part in it, I really didn't. It was Tim and Kevin, with a couple of Kevin's mates, who sorted them out. They only found the one body and that had most of the face eaten away. There was no-one to say it wasn't me. There was no question of dental records or any of that stuff - the Spanish cops just aren't bothered. You don't even need to bung them anything.

"Tim gave me some dosh and told me to get the hell out of it. He gave me enough to get to South America but I didn't see the point of spending all that money just on an air ticket, so I had a bit of a holiday first and, well, wound up here. Tim wanted Kev to stay on, and promised him a tidy inheritance, so that's what he did. I don't know whether Tim's alive or dead, to be honest.

"And that is the truth, the whole truth and nothing but the truth, your honour, so help me God."

Rupert seemed relieved to have finally unburdened himself. He could now look us both in the eye.

"Could I have some more wine, please?" he asked, reaching out his glass.

10

"He's gone," I reported.

First home, it had fallen to me to establish that Rupert had in fact departed and not just gone on an errand. Everything was neat and tidy, nothing missing. The front door key was on the kitchen table together with a note, written in pencil: "*Thanks for everything. R.*"

Beck had rung me earlier at work.

"What do you reckon?" she had wanted to know. "Is he really telling the truth or is he still hiding something?"

To all but the most cynical, Rupert had, after all the lies, finally told the truth as he saw it. But in his case, the boundary between truth and fiction was ill defined and with time he actually came to believe his lies and fantasies. It had started innocently enough with those childhood games and Rupert Bear. Then had come the story about his parents and their tragic deaths, Aunt Mary, and his job as Senior Account Manager, not to mention his adopted name, Rupert Cunningham, and the place allegedly awaiting him at Cambridge. Against this background, it was quite conceivable that he had been involved in disposing of the hit-men in Spain, even more, that he had been an accomplice in organising Gloria's murder. And all the time his sick mind had shut him off from reality and allowed him to live in a cosy world of self-delusion. Even his account of Sara's death didn't have to be true. No credence could be placed on Tim's account either - he could easily have lied to protect his lover; after all, he had nothing to lose as he waited for death.

"He's telling the truth," I uttered with a conviction I did not feel.

In a sense, it was all academic. Rupert had once more performed his now-famous vanishing trick and, despite my earlier good resolutions, I had no further desire to pursue our former quarry. Yes, I despised him, but felt no malice towards him, and was not prepared to implicate myself in any way by involving the police. For Watson and myself, the case had to be closed.

After the brief disruption of having a re-incarnated Rupert beamed in on us from beyond the grave, we determined to focus once more on our own lives. We had seen too much suffering, too much horror and anguish, too much death. Now it was time to move on and look to the future.

My friendship with Geoff was on the verge of blossoming into romance and we planned a holiday together in Thailand. But first, I invited him to accompany me on a Sunday visit to Great Langford to see Enid and the baby.

As on the morning of the accident all that time

ago, the air was crisp and clear as we drove along near-empty roads through the rolling hills, white with frost. I had wrestled long and hard with the question of whether or not to tell Geoff the full story about Rupert and Sara, Tim and Gloria, and the whole sordid business, but in the end decided against it. What would be the point of burdening him with the moral dilemma which had tormented me for so long. The time for that might come later, when the memories had faded. No, Enid would be introduced as a distant aunt and baby Rupert as her nephew.

The welcome there was in keeping with the glorious weather and Geoff and Enid got on famously. With baby he was an even greater hit, and as I watched the two of them playing, I felt the first stirrings of motherhood and knew deep down that Geoff was destined to become the father of my children.

We stayed much longer than planned and the leave-taking was quite emotional. I had to promise not to leave my next visit so long and under no circumstances to come without bringing Geoff. He too received a tearful hug from Enid who stood on the doorstep with the baby on her arm and waved until we were out of sight.

Beck too had struck up a new relationship. This time, I approved of her choice and hoped that she and David would make a go of it. Although it was too early to talk of wedding bells, I had an intuitive feeling that our cosy domestic arrangements were coming to a natural end and that new horizons beckoned. So despite my sense of foreboding and affection for Enid, not even the following letter, arriving as it did some weeks after Rupert's surprise visit, was allowed to intrude on my new-found sense of optimism and promise.

Great Langford

Hello my dears,

Guess what! My Brian has come back. Isn't that wonderful news? There he was - just standing on the doorstep. I have come home Auntie he said just like that and he loves his baby son. He plays with him all day long and he is going to get a job before he goes to Cambridge. Fancy our Brian becoming a doctor I always knew he was clever.

Do come and visit us now we are a family again but drop me a line first so I can get in a nice piece of ham specially.

Yours faithfully,

Enid Carter (Mrs.)

Also by Simon Parish

Forced retirement and a series of malicious attacks trigger off a chain of events which carry the seeds of tragedy for ex-banker George Phillips. On the trail of the perpetrators is ambitious, young local reporter, Julie Wright, who stumbles on a serious scam and inadvertently finds herself in danger…

FINAL BALANCE

A gripping story of our time

"I'm sure you are aware that banking is undergoing a period of radical change, thanks to the I.T. revolution and globalisation of the world's economies."

George wasn't quite sure what Anthony was talking about. He sat expressionless, still clutching the near-full cup of coffee which was rapidly going cold.

"Our bank isn't insensitive to the impact these developments will have on the structure of the industry and it has publicly declared its intention to become a major player now we've crossed the threshold into the new millennium. In my view, we shall not just be participants in this revolution, we shall be at the cutting edge. It promises to be an exciting time."

Anthony's voice had risen by several tones and his eyes were fixed on a distant point, somewhere above and to the right of George's head. They came back into focus and sought George's own face which remained unmoved by the prospect of this new, golden age.

"Which brings us to you, George."

ISBN 0-9538452-3-0

Also from Bolero

'In this gripping and haunting love story, Jenny Cheshire has confirmed her rich talent as a first-class storyteller.'
Award-winning journalist and author, Robert Beaumont.

ECHOES OF THE PAST

by Jenny Cheshire

Alone and emotionally scarred after the birth of her still-born baby, Nelle is shocked to find herself whisked off on holiday to the coast of Wales by Jack, a charismatic and impulsive city financier.

But as Jack soon becomes sidetracked by boats, booze and blokish behaviour, Nelle continues to be tormented by a tragic secret. And why is she so mysteriously haunted by the ruined house at the end of the bay?

When salvation arrives in the attractive but reserved shape of Brad, Nelle suddenly finds her life in great danger. In a terrifying climax, she discovers that only by learning the truth behind their troubled pasts, can she and Brad finally conquer their demons.

But will they be allowed to?

ISBN 0-9538452-0-6

Also from Bolero

READING IN THE BATH

by Astrid Klemz

A truly entertaining selection of stories from Astrid Klemz, and most of them just short enough to read before the water gets cold! Astrid writes with a light touch and her work appeals to those in need of a brief distraction from everyday life. Some will make you smile, some have an unexpected twist, all are written in a style that we have come to expect from this prize winning author.

Stories include:

No Room In The Bedsit -
It was a lovely old chair, just what she needed to make her bedsit comfortable. Unfortunately, when she got it home she found it wasn't empty...

Ghost Train -
She often heard the sound of a train, but the line had been closed for forty years.

The Cat Who Climbed Chimneys -
Mackerel liked to climb chimneys, but never realised what a devastating effect his little hobby would have on village life.

Balalaika-
When Maura bought a second-hand balalaika in a junk shop she didn't reckon on acquiring a mysterious Russian stalker into the bargain.

ISBN 0-9538452-2-2

Bolero

Crime

Mystery

Romance